CW00349124

Dark, impeccably minimalistic stories about immigrant Irish mothers and their English-born daughters. The mothers belong to the 'lost generation' of Irish workers who emigrated to England in the middle of the last century. They call Ireland 'home' and inflict old-fashioned Catholic morals on their English daughters growing up in a more liberated time and culture. Out of this tension comes a series of stories written from the perspective of several women family members, transcending these painful differences with their courageous humour and absolute refusal to look away. The stories reinforce each other and create memorable echoes, reverberating in the mind long after the book is closed.

Martina Evans
author of *Petrol* (Anvil 2012)

Read individually, these stories might seem modest: each cuts its small piece of cloth and lays it out with truthfulness, understanding and warmth. But characters recur and situations illuminate one another, so that when we read them together we find ourselves inside the story of a whole community of Irish immigrants, suddenly faced, as the protagonists are, with the tellingly displaced expectations and longings of a generation of women and their legacy to the generations that succeeded them. Maria C. McCarthy knows how to tell this complex story, and she tells it with humanity and imagination. The thoughts, speech and actions of her characters make them intensely alive.

Susan Wicks
author of *A Place to Stop* (Salt 2012)

This is a well-made and thoughtful collection of linked short stories on the theme of Irish migration. The stories are subtle and sophisticated, the characters well drawn and the world they occupy made vivid for the reader. Maria C. McCarthy handles the emotional and moving material very well, these are never mawkish or sentimental stories and the larger themes the stories inevitably touch on are implied and suggested rather than addressed directly.

Stewart Brown
author of *Tourist, Traveller, Troublemaker: Essays on Poetry*
(Peepal Tree Press 2007)

Maria C. McCarthy was born in Ewell, Surrey in 1959, and raised by Irish parents. Her Irish heritage features strongly in her poetry, stories and her columns for BBC Radio 4's *Home Truths* (written and broadcast as Maria Bradley). Her first poetry collection, *strange fruits,* was published by Cultured Llama in 2011. She has an MA with distinction in creative writing from the University of Kent. She writes in a shed at the end of her garden in a village in North Kent. Her website is www.medwaymaria.co.uk

Also by Maria C. McCarthy

strange fruits Cultured Llama (2011)
Unexplored Territory (ed.) Cultured Llama (2012)

As Long
as it Takes

For my sisters, my brothers, my daughters, the next generation – my granddaughter Caitlin – and for all the O'Halloran, McCarthy and Condon women who travelled across the water from Ireland to England. And for Bob, with love.

As Long as it Takes

Maria C. McCarthy

Cultured Llama Publishing

First published in 2014 by
Cultured Llama Publishing
11 London Road
Teynham, Sittingbourne
ME9 9QW
www.culturedllama.co.uk

ISBN 978-0-9926485-1-0

Printed in Great Britain by Lightning Source UK Ltd

Jacket design by Mark Holihan
Cover images by Maggie Drury
Copy editing by Anne-Marie Jordan
Author photo by Gareth Arnold

Contents

'Then the posters went up, at the Labour Exchange –
"JOIN THE WRENS", "JOIN THE ATS", "PLENTY
OF WORK IN ENGLAND", "COME TO ENGLAND
AND SEE THE WORLD".'

Noreen Hill
in *Across the Water: Irish Women's Lives in Britain*

As Long as it Takes

The dust took months to settle. Every time I polished the furniture, it was covered again within a couple of hours, like salt sprinkled on an icy path.

Bill had taken a sledgehammer to the brown-tiled surround in the living room and built in a York stone fireplace. We kept the old mirror, a wedding present from Bill's mother, and hung it on the chimney breast. You know that saying *she's not herself?* That's how it was when I looked in that mirror, wondering who the woman was that stared back through the dust.

I started to go into the baby's room whilst Bill was at work. I'd stand at the end of the cot, threading my fingers through the holes of the blanket that my friend Maura had crocheted. Bill found me in there early one evening when I should have been making the dinner. I'd lost track of time, shaking out the folded nappies, refolding them, ironing the smocks, dusting the tins of talc, bottles of baby lotion, tubs of zinc and castor oil, all with the seals unbroken. 'It's time we put a stop to this,' he said, and he ripped the cot apart with big, angry moves, like when he'd knocked out the fireplace, and he made a bonfire in the garden. I stood on the back step and watched the flames, lighting the next cigarette as soon as I'd finished the one before, leaning against the doorframe until my shoulder went numb.

The next morning's post brought two items: a letter from home, and a parcel wrapped in brown paper with the required number of stamps and sufficient coarse string to hold it together. Nonetheless, it had been delayed by several weeks. Inside, a yellowing christening gown last worn by my brother Sean, and a note in my mother's careful handwriting: *Sorry I can't be there. God bless.* I lifted the gown by the shoulders, shook it softly, cradled it across my arms, and draped it over the back of the kitchen chair. I lit a ciggy before tackling the letter, postmarked a few days before. It was from Sean. He made brief mention of my 'troubles' before moving on to the latest news on Mother's state of health. I ground my cigarette into the curved edge of the ashtray, then lifted the christening gown from the back of chair, replacing it in the brown paper in the same folds that it arrived in, closing the flaps of the parcel, knotting the string. I carried it upstairs, lifted the suitcase from the top of the wardrobe, and laid the parcel in the bottom of the case, burying it beneath the clothes and shoes as I packed.

The night before I left for Ireland, Bill heaved away on top of me as if I wasn't there, his head buried in my shoulder. And I lay still as he cried afterwards, big shuddering sobs on my useless chest, where the child should have been nursing.

Bill saw me as far as the ticket barrier at Euston. 'I don't know when I'll be back,' I said, picking a stray thread from the lapel of his jacket. 'You know how it is. A dying woman takes as long as she takes.'

He smiled; wrinkles puckered at the corners of his eyes. I wanted to raise my fingers to them, smooth them away. 'You'll be back when you're ready,' he said, and squeezed my hand before passing me the suitcase. I watched his broad shoulders as he turned, leaving well before the train was due to pull out.

The ship, The Hibernian, was more suitable for carrying cattle than people. There weren't enough seats for everyone in second-class, whole families exposed to the elements with only wooden benches to perch on, children balanced on bags and cases on the deck amid the pools of vomit. I hugged the rails, skulking round the edge of the ship, moving on if anyone had a mind to smile or speak to me. I could feel a rise and fall in the pit of my belly. I placed one foot on the lower rail, and climbed up to the second; the wind blew so hard it felt like my teeth would be shaken out from the roots. I leaned over and spewed a thin gruel of tea with lumps of the egg and cress sandwiches I'd eaten on the train. I reached into my handbag for a hankie to wipe my mouth. That's when I saw her, a small child, three or four years of age, picking her way around sleeping, stretched-out legs. She toddled around like a drunk, swinging this way and that. She was no bigger than Brendan, Maura's boy.

I'd taken him in that spring when Maura went into hospital. I decorated the room before he arrived, pale blue. It hadn't been changed since I lost the first child. There were no scans in those days, you had to wait and see, so the room was painted lemon. I'd prayed for a boy, and that was what I lost, seven months gone, nothing to do but go through with it, though he was already dead. I never got to see him: taken away and thrown in the hospital incinerator; no picture to hold in my mind of what he looked like; no grave to visit to mourn my child.

Brendan was gorgeous. I could have eaten him for dinner. Dimpled, with red hair and freckles; he could have passed for mine. I slipped him sweets and titbits, bathed him, and cuddled him up in a fluffy towel. I loved to smell his hair after I'd washed it in Silvikrin Green Apple shampoo – just like him, a ripening fruit – and I'd tickle his squashy tummy until he giggled, then into his pyjamas for a bedtime story. He hadn't that sort of attention at home, with the five of them.

When Maura came out of hospital, I offered to keep him for a while. She wasn't too good; wouldn't say what had gone on, just that there would be no more children. You'd think it would be a relief, she'd more than she could cope with, and her Jack, God love him, wasn't much cop as a father. He could make them, all right, but after that... the drink always came first.

So it would have been for the best if Brendan stayed with me, but Bill wasn't so keen. 'You're spoiling that child,' he said, when he found the new clothes I'd bought, and when I gave him a proper World Cup football. 'Sure, he's barely big enough to handle a beach ball. What does he want with a leather one?' And I suppose he was right. Kieran, Maura's oldest, got hold of it: kicking and scuffing it around the street with his mates.

Brendan stopped coming around after a while. Maura said it wasn't fair to give him presents; the others would get jealous. I saw less of her as spring turned to summer, and when I did see her, it was like she wasn't listening, just staring into the distance. I missed Maura. I'd other friends, but none as close as we'd been. I'd wander around the town alone, all dressed up and nowhere to go, stopping for a milky coffee, chatting with whoever might be at the next table. But the English girls, they look at you strange if you try to strike up a conversation, like you've escaped from the asylum. There was a girl with a baby and toddler in the Kings Shade Walk Café. 'You look like you could do with a hand,' I said. She was struggling with shopping, and trying to keep her coffee cup away from the grabbing hands of the toddler. I picked him up and put him on my lap, breaking off a bit of my toast for him. Jesus, I've never seen a woman move so fast.

'I can manage, thank you,' she said, snatching the child, turning her back on me, more content with the whinging of the two children than my company.

I walked across the deck towards the girl, and lifted her to sit on my hip. 'Where's your mammy, then?' I said, and we wandered around until she wriggled from my side, reaching towards a sleeping woman, two children draped around her and a dented pile of coats on the deck, where the smallest one had slept.

I shook the mother awake, 'Is this little lady yours?'

'Siobhan!' she said and pulled her close. 'She's a devil for staying awake; fights sleep every step of the way. She nodded off, so I took a chance and caught forty winks myself.' The child was squirming to get down, and the mother with big dark circles beneath her eyes. I looked around, and I saw many more like her, mothers with four, five, six children, luggage, coats and cardigans, and no men around to help.

I made myself useful for the rest of the crossing, holding Siobhan whilst her mother slept – Anne-Marie her name was – taking the older ones to the toilets, getting us hot drinks from the tea bar. And we travelled on together from Dun Laoghaire, on the train to Limerick, parting at the rail station. She went on to County Clare, and I set off for Mother's.

She had her boys around her, gathered like a scene from an old film. Her lips were sunken, her teeth in a glass on the night stand. Her skin was yellow, dotted with pale brown patches, like her freckles had joined together. Her hair was in need of a brush – not the sort of thing a man would think of.

I took a breath and breezed in, as cheerful as I could be. 'What's the story, getting me over here when there's not a thing wrong with you?' I plumped up her pillows, hauled her up to sitting, tying her bed jacket where the ribbon had come loose.

'Will you ever stop fussing,' she said. 'Get me a drop of that water.' Sean held a tumbler to her lips. Liam kind of nodded in my direction – never much of a one for words. He disappeared into the kitchen, and soon there was the familiar whistle of the kettle and the rattling of teacups on the old tin tray.

I followed Liam into the kitchen. I picked at the loaf on the side. I hadn't eaten since the day before, yet my stomach felt tight, and I wasn't sure if I could get a crumb down my throat. Liam had laid out three cups; I lifted a fourth cup from the press. It was marked with brown stains, and blobs of sugar stuck to the bottom. 'She can only take water now,' Liam said, taking it from my hand. Our fingers touched. He looked at me for a second, then his mouth crumpled and he turned his back as he stirred the teapot. He'd appeared older than his years for as long as I could remember, but now the lines were deeper, and his once-black hair was threaded with silver.

'She's drifted off,' Sean said, pulling a third chair to the table. He scooped sugar into his cup, and stirred it for longer than necessary. 'You can have my room, Joan. I'll go in with Liam.'

'Grand.' As the tea hit the back of my throat I felt a wave of exhaustion. 'I'll go and lie down then, so.'

As I lay on the narrow bed I felt the roll of the ship, the waves starting at my toes, rushing to my head, then sweeping down to my feet again. I remembered the days before I left for England, assembling the clothes and shoes to fit a single suitcase: two of everything. Packing and re-packing, listening to Mother's speech, repeated several times a day, not knowing how she'd manage, 'with your poor father gone.' I recalled the turn of her head as I left, unable to see me to the door, unwilling to wish me well.

A fine, meaty smell rose through the house. Liam tapped on the door and placed a cup of tea on the bedside table. 'There's some lamb stew heated up from yesterday. You'll have a plate then, so?'

'I will. Give me five minutes, and I'll look in on Mother.'

Her eyes were closed, but there was nothing wrong with her hearing. 'You took your time coming over from England,' she said, as soon as I crossed the threshold of her room.

'I didn't at all. Sure, it's only days since I got the letter, and I'd things to sort out at home.'

'What things would they be?' She pronounced the word 'things' as if she were spitting out something sour. 'You've only himself to look after.'

'He has to have something to eat in the house, even if it's only eggs and rashers.' But she wasn't listening; she'd slipped away again, so I went downstairs for my dinner.

The stew was good and hearty. I cleared my plate and Sean dipped the ladle into the pot to refill it. I didn't re-fuse. 'She took it hard about the babies, God rest their souls,' he said. He made the sign of the cross. Liam cleared his throat, looked sideways at Sean. A silence fell as we finished the last of the stew, the light fading through the kitchen window.

'I'll look in on Mother,' Liam said after a while.

I clattered the plates into the sink, and held up a tea towel that had seen better days. 'I'll wash, you wipe,' I said to Sean. There was a look of protest on his face. 'Sure, you look like you did as a child when you were asked to fetch the wood, or do anything at all.' He broke into a grin and flicked me with the tea towel. I filled the sink with hot water from the kettle on the range. 'So, are you courting?'

'There was someone, but...'

'Ah, a handsome man like you, there's plenty of girls.' I nudged him with my elbow. He dropped his head to his chest, his cheeks reddening.

'You know how it is with Mammy.'

'Yes, I know how it is.'

I hung my black costume and good white blouse on a wooden hanger in the wardrobe. At the bottom of my suitcase the christening gown lay in its brown paper with the knotted string, cradled between my black shoes and my make-up bag. The paper crackled as I lifted it, just as when it had been parcelled at the kitchen table below, the string cut with her good scissors, the small lined notepad taken from the drawer.

I passed Liam on the landing at midnight, him on his way to bed, me to sit with Mother. A rosary was draped over a statue of Our Lady on the night stand, hands joined, fingers pointing Heavenwards, her perfect features serene in eternal suffering. I sat with the parcel on my lap, my fingers playing with the knotted string, the room lit by the soft glow of a small lamp. Mother's body looked twisted, and she grimaced as she shifted, so I took a pillow and placed it under her arm. There was little flesh left between skin and bone. I reached across with a pillow for the other arm. Her brow wrinkled, then relaxed. 'What's that?' she said, looking to where the parcel lay, within reach of her hand.

'I've brought the gown back,' I said.

'Ah, you'll be needing it soon enough.'

'No, Mother, I won't.'

Her lips were dry and cracked. I lifted her head, and held the glass to her mouth. It took all her strength to swallow. 'Don't be talking like that,' she said. 'You'll keep trying.'

'No, Mother. Bill and I just have to accept…We can't go through all that again.'

She pressed her lips into a line, her eyes flickering beneath closed lids. 'You can and you will.'

'No, Mother.'

She winced as I raised my voice as if every sense was working overtime, the dim light too much for her eyes, the sound of my words too harsh for her ears. 'It's a woman's life. What else will you do if you don't have children?'

The boys and I stood by the coffin as the people of the village paid their respects, each shaking our hands and finding some good words for the dead woman. I dreamt that night of a never-ending procession of hands in black sleeves, squeezing my hand until it too worked free from my body, and I left it clasping the hands of the mourners while I crept into the darkness.

I scrubbed the house from top to bottom, and bundled up Mother's clothes, making good use of the folded squares of brown paper in the kitchen drawer. I sat with the small pad of notepaper and a pile of envelopes, wrote to those who needed to be told, and thanked those that had helped at the wake.

The boys walked me to the bus stop. 'Now you'll give that kitchen a lick of paint, and if the house gets too much, get Molly Ryan to give it a clean once a week.' I gave Sean a good hug, and got a firm squeeze of the hand from Liam. 'You'll come and visit us in England. Stay a while.'

'When the farm allows,' Liam said.

'Sean, you'll come, stay longer. Let the English girls have a look at you.'

He waved my comment away, grinning all the while. 'Maybe you'll be blessed by then,' he said.

I leaned against the window of the bus and watched the fields and towns through the drizzle. The glass was cold and it rattled a rhythm through my skull, never still, never quiet, faster, higher, a steady hum, then dropping down the scale, the bus shivering as it loaded and unloaded its charges. As the bus emptied at Limerick, I remained with my cheek pressed to the glass. It was still now, just the bustle of the bus station below the window.

'This is as far as we go, unless you want to go back where you came from.' The driver tipped his cap to the back of his head. There was a dent across his forehead, the skin whiter above than below.

'No, I don't want to go back,' I said, but made no move to rise.

'Come on now, you can't stay on the bus.' He handed me my handbag from the seat beside me, and I followed him out to the side of the bus where he unloaded my case from the luggage space. I stared at the case on the pavement. 'It won't walk by itself,' he said. He picked it up. 'So I'll take it along to the café at the railway station, and see if you follow it.'

'Now, it's nothing fancy here,' he said, placing a cup of tea in front of me, 'but they'll do you a sandwich or a fry.' I listened as he chattered on the other side of the table. He might as well have been talking Chinese for all I took in, but it was comfort enough, the company and the drone of his voice, and the badge on the front of his cap to focus on as it lay on the table. 'I'm away now, but Norah will look after you, won't you, Norah?' A large woman with frizzy red hair and a tea towel draped over her shoulder nodded in my direction. The badge and the cap disappeared from the table, and the talking stopped.

I sat all afternoon, smoking, drinking cup after cup of

tea. Norah brought poached eggs, and I managed a few mouthfuls, though I gained no taste or pleasure from them. The boat train was announced and left, and I stayed, my case tucked under the table. Norah emptied the ashtray for the second time, wiping it round with a grey cloth. 'If you're that keen on this place, I'll put you to work,' she said. I took her at her word, and began to clear tables and wipe them down.

There was a room that Norah knew of, not far from the café: a single bed, bare walls except for a crucifix, a wardrobe and a chair. I did nothing to enhance it, the only sign of inhabitance my clothes in the wardrobe and my shoes at the side of the bed at night. The summer passed in the spitting of fat, the steam from the tea urn, and wiping crumbs and spilt sugar from the tables. July turned to August, and September was approaching on the day that Anne-Marie came in with her brood. The children, God love 'em, were talking with Irish accents that'd fade soon enough when they were back in their English schools, once their lips had forgotten the taste of Tayto crisps and red lemonade.

'So you didn't go back, after your mother...' Anne-Marie said.

'Sure, what have I got back there?' I ruffled each of the little ones' hair in turn, and them ducking away from my hand in the way that kids do.

She stopped her teacup at her lips and placed it back in the saucer. 'Honest to God, Joan, they'll be frantic back home. And what about the old man? He'll think you've left him.' I wiped the next table, clearing the plate before the women there had finished her last mouthful. 'Have you left him, Joan?' I wouldn't look at her, carried on with my work, but she wouldn't stop giving out. 'For God's sake, Joan, you've got to go back.'

I didn't take it in at the time, but as I lay in bed that night, the words went over and over in my head: *He'll* think *you've left him… have you left him?* And in the way that people do when they're rehearsing for a play. *Have* you left him? Have *you* left him? Have you *left* him? Have you left *him?*

But in Limerick, no-one knew me as Joan, the woman who'd lost three babies; I was Joan who served up sausage, egg and rashers. And they were passing through, on their way to somewhere else. So I carried on frying, buttering, and pouring tea.

The rain came down in torrents the first week of September. It sounds stupid, but what turned me around was the lack of a warm jumper and a good raincoat. I only had light clothes with me when I arrived at the end of July, and as the autumn chill arrived one Monday morning, I searched for my mustard sweater before realising that it was in the bottom drawer of my dressing table back home. I thought of the new raincoat I'd bought at C&A in the spring sale and my good umbrella that wouldn't turn inside out in the wind.

I sat on the edge of the bed in my little room and cried for the lack of an autumn wardrobe, for the mirror above the fireplace that Bill had built, for the cot that he'd burnt in the garden, for the romper suits that went to the jumble sale to clothe someone else's child. I cried for Bill, for my babies and, finally, I cried for myself: big, mascara-stained tears mixed with the drippings from my nose, falling unwiped onto my skirt.

I brought down my case from the top of the wardrobe. The parcel with the christening gown was still in there, and I slipped it into a Dunnes Stores carrier.

The sun was setting on the bay as I arrived for the crossing, and a damp breeze ruffled my hair as I walked the gangplank. I could see the dark water swirling below through the gaps between the planks. I found a place at the back of the ship, looking back on the bay as we pulled away from my homeland. I lifted the parcel from the carrier, untied the string and cradled the gown across my arms. I traced my fingers over the greying lace, the satin ribbon threaded through the bodice, peeping out then disappearing.

And it slipped from my fingers to the waves below, fluttering, dancing, riding the foam, appearing, disappearing.

A Tea Party

The baby smells of the milk that Mum leaves on the windowsill to go sour for making scones. Mum takes the nappy to the bucket in the bathroom, scrapes the poo into the toilet with a knife then sticks it in to soak. Sometimes I stir the nappies around with the big wooden tongs that Mum uses to lift the washing from the twin tub. Deeter Doh-er, Deeter Doh-er, clunking and chunking, Deeter Doh-er, then she lifts the steaming nappies into the sink to rinse off the bubbles, and then into the spin dryer. It starts slow then screeches faster and faster, like a rocket ship taking off, and the twin tub dances across the floor, clunk-a, clunk-a. Mum lifts the lid and the clothes are pinned to the side, like the people on that ride when the funfair came to Epsom Downs.

They're turning slower now. I want to put my hand in and feel what the clothes are feeling, dizzy, but I mustn't stick my fingers in or I'll end up like that man in the corner shop who has a finger that stops halfway. We must pray for him, like when I prayed to get a kitten. Praying doesn't always get you what you want, but you have to do it just in case, or horrible things might happen, like dying with a sin on your soul. That's why babies have to be baptised, to get rid of Original Sin. The priest washes it off with holy water. It's like washing poo off the nappies, except you can't put a baby in the washing machine, so the priest has to do it. He makes the sign of the cross on the baby's forehead with his thumb. That puts God in. God is in the priest's thumb.

Babies can't swim, so they only have the water on their head. I can nearly swim. I've been going to Epsom Baths with the school. We walk there in a crocodile, two by two, holding hands, and I'm always paired with Susan Saunders. There are four Susans in my class and five Catherines, but they are all called something different: two Cathys, One Kate, one Katie and a Catherine.

Uncle Michael doesn't live with us any more, now the new baby is here, as there isn't room. He's in digs now. Digs is where a lady cooks you breakfast and dinner, but you're not allowed to watch telly with her, only go in the kitchen for meals, and you have to pay her so much a week, and you get a bedroom. Sometimes all to yourself and sometimes with other men who might be friends or you might not even know them. Uncle Michael doesn't like it in digs. He meets Dad in the White Horse after work, and they stay there all evening, so he doesn't have to go back too early. Dad hardly ever comes home for his dinner these days; he goes straight to the pub. He doesn't say prayers with us either, as he's not there at bedtime, though sometimes he does and he brings back crisps and lemonade from the White Horse and bars of Cadbury's Dairy Milk that Charlie keeps behind the bar for when we play in the pub garden. There's something in the 'Our Father' about crisps: *give us our crisps as we forgive them that trespass against us.* It's the prayer that makes our father give us crisps, so Maggie and me keep saying it, even though Dad isn't there to help us.

Sometimes I wait and wait for Dad's donkey jacket to be on its hook in the hall and it's not there when I go to bed, and it's not there when I get up in the morning 'cause he's already gone to work.

Uncle Michael was funny when he first came over – that's what they call it when someone comes on the boat from Ireland: 'coming over'. He came back with us when we'd been 'home' on holiday – that's what Mum calls it, going home. His mouth was hanging open when we got off the train at Euston, and he was staring. You don't get that many people in one place where he lived, in Ennistymon. Mum told him to stop catching flies, and did he want people to think he was bog Irish? Some people think Irish people aren't very clever, and you mustn't give them any ammunition.

He used to say hello to everyone in the street, like they do in Ireland, but Mum told him people don't do that in England, and he'd end up in Long Grove, which is the loony bin where she used to work before having us.

Uncle Michael gave me a tea set for my birthday. It has pink and blue flowers on it. There are little slots in the cardboard box for the saucers, and they stand upright, but slanting forwards, and there are round holes to put the cups in. There aren't any spoons. It's the best present I've ever had, but I didn't get to keep it nice for long. I got called to dinner, and left the tea set on the floor, and Brendan broke a cup. He cried, as he'd cut his finger on a sharp bit, then I cried when I saw what he'd done, and Mum got cross and told me to stop making such a racket as I'd set the baby off, and didn't she have enough to worry about without an old teacup. It wasn't old at all.

Brendan didn't even get smacked, as he's only two, and I have to make allowances for him. I had a pain in my tummy when Mum threw the broken bits in the bin. I hate Brendan. I pinched him hard when no-one was looking, then Mum got cross with him when he cried too long and set the baby off again. Crying just makes grown-ups angry; it never seems to be all right to cry.

I have tea parties with Maggie, and sometimes with Sindy and my teddies. I pretend to be Mum, and Maggie is Auntie Joan, and we talk like they do when Mum gets the Maxwell House out of the cupboard: about the other mums and aunties, and what Dr Evans has to say about Auntie Joan's trouble downstairs. I don't always understand what they're talking about, but if I ask I get sent out to play. I like listening to grown-up ladies, and seeing their bosoms when they've got babies with them. Bosom is a funny word. It sounds like it feels, all squashy and soft and smelling of talcum powder, like Mum's. The baby sucks it, and I get to see it when it's just us, or Auntie Pam and Auntie Joan, but not when Dad's around, or Uncle Bill or Uncle Dave. Men don't get to see bosoms, only ladies, children and babies.

Auntie Pam has a baby, but Auntie Joan doesn't have any, even though she's married. You can't have babies until you get married, God doesn't let you. Some people have lots of babies and some have none at all, even though they like them a lot. I don't know why God won't let Auntie Joan have a baby. She holds Brendan really tight sometimes, and she likes to cuddle the new baby. Mum doesn't look very happy if she holds them for too long.

Mum doesn't cuddle me much these days; she's too busy. Auntie Joan doesn't cuddle me either – she prefers boys and tiny babies. I like girls best 'cause they don't break things. On the night the lady brought the baby, the fat lady with the clock on her bosom, Maggie and me were arguing about whether she'd brought a boy or a girl. She looked like a shadow puppet, standing in the doorway of our bedroom with the hall light behind her, and she told us to be quiet 'cause Mum was resting. Auntie Joan came in the morning and she asked the fat lady what kind of baby it was, and she said a girl, and Auntie Joan said, 'Never mind.' Auntie Joan did the ironing when Mum was resting. She held Brendan's shorts up to her face and smelled them and rubbed them against her cheek. Her eyes were red, and her face looked like a scrunched-up paper bag.

When Maggie had her first Holy Communion, she had a new white dress with a skirt underneath made of scratchy stuff to make the dress stick out. The dress was silky with sewing on it, so you could feel the flowers and leaves stitched onto it. I closed my eyes and traced the flowers with my fingertips. I had to wash my hands first.

She had a hair band with pretend pink flowers on it, and white hairgrips to hold the veil in place. Mum said the outfit cost a fortune, but it will do for me when I have my first Holy Communion. Uncle Michael gave Maggie a white prayer book, but it's not as good as the tea set he gave me. A prayer book is only for one person – it's not for sharing – and you can't play with a prayer book.

I wore one of Maggie's old dresses, the one with stamps from all over the world printed on it. Dad prodded my tummy and said I looked like a parcel. I do like that dress, but it would have been nice to have a new one. Brendan gets new clothes all the time 'cause Kieran's clothes are too big to hand down, and Auntie Joan buys him bits and bobs too.

I held Dad's hand as we walked down the aisle, and I sat next to him, just me, as he was at the end of the row. He was wearing a suit, light grey, and a maroon tie that Mum had chosen at Burton's. Mum said that he couldn't go to a first Holy Communion in his work clothes, looking like he'd been dressed from the ragbag.

He'd been moaning about the baby before we left, saying couldn't Mum shut her up. Mum said he was keen enough to make them, but didn't want to know afterwards. He went quiet and they were staring at each other, him standing at the door, her at the sink, then Maggie walked into the kitchen in her dress and his face went soft again, and Brendan went charging at her, clinging onto her legs. It was like when you're waiting for a train and the gap between the platforms makes you feel dizzy, then trains come from different directions, and when they stop, the space doesn't feel so scary; you're just caught up in the excitement of where you're going.

The day of Maggie's first Holy Communion was the first time I'd seen Dad all week. The Sunday before, I'd had him all to myself at 11 o'clock Mass, as Maggie and Kieran had been to the 8 o'clock one, and Brendan was playing up so he stayed home with Mum and the baby. The leaves were piled up in the park on the way to church, and Dad lifted me high so that I could kick the top of the hills of leaves and feel like I was walking on them, like when Jesus walked on water. Mum doesn't let me kick the leaves in my good shoes; I'm surprised she lets me walk in them at all.

After Mass he took me to Stebbings. I chose a pink sugar mouse and he said not to tell the others, it's our secret. I sucked the sugar until all that was left was the string tail, and then Dad wiped my mouth with his my hankie.

Mrs Roberts caught up with us – she had been to the 11 o'clock too. We walked her home, even though it was out of our way. She laughed every time Dad spoke, like she'd heard a funny joke.

'You'll come in for a cuppa and a slice of cake,' she said as we reached her gate. She offered me Victoria sponge, fondant fancies and iced fairy cakes with little silver balls on top. Her long red fingernails curled round the plate as she held it out to me and, as she leant over, I could see the line where her bosoms met. I chose a fairy cake, but the silver balls were too hard to crunch, so I spat them out onto the plate. There was no silver then, just white.

She let me play tea parties with her big teapot, cups and saucers: her best china. She said I could play with what I liked as long as I didn't tell anyone that we'd been there. 'Is it a deal?' she said; I couldn't speak because I had cake in my mouth.

Dad and Mrs Roberts went away to talk about grown-up things. It was a bit funny as men and ladies don't usually talk together; the men talk to the men and the ladies talk to the ladies, especially after they get married. I think they talk and hold hands before they get married, but all that stops after they get babies.

Mrs Roberts came back into the kitchen, smiling with her bright red lips. She looked at me and laughed. 'We can't send you home like that,' she said, and she wiped my face with a tea towel, her face close to mine. Her mouth is too red. I can see it when I close my eyes. It's like the felt pen that Brendan got on the living room carpet that wouldn't come out.

Auntie Pam said something that Mum didn't like. She said that you shouldn't refuse your husband, as 'they seem to need it more than we do and they'll go elsewhere if they don't get it from us.' I think it's because Dad didn't come home for his dinner yesterday. Mum left his plate on top of a saucepan of hot water with another plate on top, upside down; it looked like a flying saucer. No donkey jacket in the hall at bedtime, and lamb chops, mashed potatoes, gravy and peas, all thick and gooey, scraped into the bin. Today, Mum didn't make him dinner. He could have gone to Uncle Michael's digs to eat, I suppose, but I don't think Mum likes the idea of another lady cooking for Dad.

I was woken up by voices and banging. Mum said, 'There's no point talking to you when you're three sheets to the wind,' and I couldn't understand what Dad said. I climbed into bed with Maggie and cuddled up to her back. Then the baby started crying. Dad said something about the bloody baby, and then it sounded like something was knocked over, and Mum said, 'Eejit, you'll wake up all the children,' and he said, 'There's no peace in this house since that baby.' His voice sounded like Maggie's talking doll when the battery ran out.

I wanted to tell Maggie that I had cake at Mrs Roberts', but I couldn't because it's a secret and, anyway, she was tied up with her precious prayer book. So I took out the tea set and sat Sindy, Big Ted and Little Ted on the floor. I pretended to pour from the teapot, and I used the spare saucer to serve up cake. I made Victoria sponge and fondant fancies out of plasticine, though I couldn't get the colour right, as it had all been rolled into one brown ball.

'Will you have a cup of tea, Jack?' Sindy said. She leaned over so Big Ted could see where I'd pulled down her top to show the line where her bosoms meet. 'And some orange squash for the little one.' She poured a drink for little Ted. 'Would you like Victoria sponge, fondant fancies or iced fairy cakes with little silver balls on top?' Little Ted took a fairy cake. 'And now we must go and talk about grown-up things. Come on, Jack.'

'Thank you, Mrs Roberts,' Big Ted said. I lifted Sindy and Big Ted onto the bed. Little Ted dropped his fairy cake on the carpet.

Mum stood in the doorway with the baby on her hip. She didn't say anything; she just stood there.

Later, she cooked Birds Eye Cod in Batter, boiled potatoes, peas and carrots. She made a flying saucer with Dad's dinner plate, and set it on a pan of water. She didn't do the washing-up; she slid down in an armchair in front of the telly. We watched *Coronation Street,* then *World in Action,* and it was only when Brendan fell asleep on the floor that she remembered to send us to bed. I said the 'Our Father' with Maggie, and I prayed in my head that Dad would come home for his Birds Eye Cod in Batter, and not go to another lady's house for dinner. I lay in bed until I heard the click of his key and his boot against the door; it sticks unless you push it hard. I heard his footsteps in the hall, and waited for Mum to say something, but all was quiet except for his breathing as he passed our bedroom door.

There was a pub smell on the stairs. I trod carefully, missing the creaky step, and stood by the living room door, which was almost shut. I pressed my face to the gap. There was a black and white film on the telly; a lady and a man were kissing. Mum was staring at the fire; the coal had gone grey with tiny bits of orange trying to shine through.

Gillian's Dolls

Sharon bit into a meat paste triangle and stared at the Russian dolls that stood high on a shelf in Gillian's kitchen. They were closed up tight. Sharon had seen a set in the raffle at the church bazaar, lined up in height order. She'd watched as the lady arranged the prizes, twisting each doll, top part one way, bottom part another, then a smaller one poked its head out, and on and on, right down to the fifth that was the size of a monkey nut. There could be another inside that; it was just a case of waiting until it cracked open, like when a chick pokes its beak through an egg.

There were thin slices of Battenburg after the sandwiches. Sharon peeled off the icing and ate the pink squares first, the yellow ones last. 'You can go and play in the bedroom now,' Gillian's mum said. Sharon wanted to ask about the dolls, but felt too shy in front of Gillian's mum. She practised the words in her head as she climbed the stairs behind Gillian. Finally, the words came out as she sat on the bed, stringing a loop of wool between her hands.

'Can we play with your Russian dolls?'

'They're not for playing with, they're for looking at.'

'What?'

'My gran gave them to me when I was a baby. Don't you have things that are nice to keep, just to look at?' Gillian looked at her, and broke into a smile.

Sharon pulled her thumb through the wool and caught the strands at the back to make a cat's cradle. 'Yeah, of course,' she said. She had one gran that lived in Ireland and another that lived in Heaven. Neither of them sent presents.

As Gillian hunted for the Cluedo game in the wooden toy box under the window, Silky, her kitten, wandered into the bedroom. Sharon had prayed for a kitten, the best part of a novena. That's what you did when you wanted something, but her mum said the dog and the rabbit were quite enough. Silky scratched at the frayed threads of a white satin hair ribbon that poked out from beneath the bed; Gillian's ribbon that had tied her long blond hair, brushed and shiny in its tight ponytail. Sharon dangled the ribbon before Silky, pulling it out of reach before his claws could catch it. She tucked it up the sleeve of her cardigan.

When it was time to go, Gillian's mum said, 'You're welcome anytime, dear.' She didn't look at Sharon when she said it. She was standing at the kitchen sink with a tumbler of water. She tipped a blue pill from her hand into her mouth, throwing her head back as she swallowed.

'Let's get you home, ginger nut,' Gillian's dad said, rubbing Sharon's head. Her dad did the head-rubbing thing too, though sometimes he went through all of their names, including the boys, until he got to the right one.

How's it going, Maggie, Janice, Brendan, Kieran, Sharon. And she would say *Da-a-ad*, long and drawn out, and he would say: *Sure, I'm only teasing. I knew it was you all the time* and rub her head, making her hair into a worse mess than it was already. At least her dad remembered her name in the end. She wanted to say: *My name's Sharon, not ginger nut,* but it was rude to answer back to a grown-up.

Sharon wove the ribbon in and out of her fingers as she walked through the back door into the kitchen. All the cooker rings were on the go, four saucepans bubbling, the windows steamed up, and her mum's face was as red as the kitchen table-top.

'Get the knives and forks out, will you, Sharon.'

Sharon went to the drawer, and counted out seven of everything. 'Mum, can I have a pogo stick? Gillian's got one and I'm really good at it.'

'If we all had what Gillian had…' her mum said, spearing slices of lamb with a long, two-pronged fork, and counting them out onto the plates. 'Do you want some dinner, or did you have enough to eat at Gillian's?'

'Yes, please, a little bit.'

Sharon carried the knives and forks through to the living room, and dropped them in a pile on the table. 'Did you have a nice time?' Maggie asked, keeping her eyes on the screen where Meg Richardson was in the kitchen of the Crossroads Motel, discussing menus with Carlos the chef.

'Yes, thanks. Gillian's got these Russian dolls. You know the ones that sit inside each other, but she's not allowed to play with them; they're just for looking at.'

'That's weird,' said Maggie, scratching at her nails with an emery board.

Amy Turtle was flicking round reception with a feather duster, listening in to the conversation between Diane, the receptionist, and Vince, the postman. Two guests nodded and smiled as Diane passed them their keys. 'They have a lot of dumb guests at that motel,' Maggie said.

Sharon looked for a space on the sofa. It was full of Janice, Brendan and Kieran. You could get four on there if you tried, but Janice had tucked her legs up and Kieran slouched sideways. She set out the knives and forks as her mum shouted, 'Dinner,' from the kitchen. They filed out to collect their plates, Sharon first. If she ate fast she could get a seat on the sofa.

'Gillian's mum said I'm welcome anytime,' she said, as she picked up her dinner plate from the kitchen table.

'As long as you don't make a nuisance of yourself,' her mum said, flicking the ash of her cigarette into the sink.

Gillian's gabardine mac hung above Sharon's hook in the cloakroom. It smelt new, like the clothes at C&A. Sharon's mac had been handed down from Maggie, the same as her skirt, blouse and cardigan. She slipped her arms into the sleeves of the other girl's coat. It was tight. Sharon's mum said she was pleasantly plump. Gillian was slim; not surprising living on meat paste sandwiches, you wouldn't get plump on those. She slipped her hands into the pockets. There was a pair of woollen mittens and a blue-edged hankie with forget-me-nots embroidered in one corner.

At home that afternoon, Sharon pulled the hankie from the waistband of her skirt. She rubbed the soft cotton on her cheeks as she lay on her candlewick bedspread with the handkerchief spread on her face, breathing through the fabric. It made her fingers tingle and the blood rush to her head, like when she did handstands in gym class.

The back door slammed, and Sharon jumped up at the sound of footsteps on the stairs. She stuffed the hankie inside her pillowcase.

Maggie grunted. This meant hello. 'You're up to something,' she said, dropping her bag onto her bed.

'So are you, I know what time you came in last night.'

'If you say anything, you're dead.'

'S'alright. Mum was asleep in the armchair before the *Nine O'Clock News*. Bet she didn't wake up 'til God Save the Queen.'

'Be upstanding for the Queen!' Maggie said. They stood and saluted, and fell onto their beds, laughing.

'So, who were you with last night: a boy? Mmm.' Sharon kissed the back of her own hand, making slurping sounds.

'His name is Simon if you must know.' Maggie blushed and smiled like the ladies in the soppy films that their mum liked.

'Ooh, Simon.' Sharon made smacking noises with her lips.

'Yeah, I'm seeing him again on Saturday, but don't tell Mum.'

Once Maggie had gone downstairs, Sharon hid the handkerchief in the shoebox beneath her bed along with Gillian's hair ribbon. It was a safe place for secret things since her mum had decided that Maggie and Sharon were big enough to tidy their own room.

At dinner, Sharon told her mum that Gillian was in the Guides. 'There's room for new girls to join. Gillian says I can go this Friday to see what it's like.'

'Hmm,' her mum said, 'it's very nice for Gillian's mum to be able to afford the uniform and to have the time to walk her down to the church hall on a Friday night just when the dinner needs cooking.'

'But, Mum, Gillian goes to Guides and ballet and horse riding. I don't do anything.'

'You've your brothers and sisters to play with. Gillian's on her own. You should count your blessings.'

Gillian was friends with Susan now. It was better, in some ways, with three – for French skipping and the like – but, in some ways, it was worse. Gillian and Susan went to ballet together and to the stables for riding lessons. Susan said her dad was going to buy her a pony, and not even for her birthday or Christmas. Sharon didn't know what to say when they talked about horses. Her dad liked to watch them racing on the telly, to take a bet on them, but it didn't seem right to mention that.

On the day that Gillian handed out the invitations to her birthday party, both Sharon and Susan went to tea at her house. 'It could be a ballet party,' Susan said, spinning around the bedroom. 'Then we could wear our dancing clothes.'

'Perhaps not,' said Gillian, 'It doesn't say it on the invitations. Besides, what would...' she paused a second and glanced at Sharon, '...the boys wear?'

Susan and Gillian practised ballet positions in the bedroom as Sharon looked on. She slipped her foot into one of Gillian's dancing shoes and tied the ribbon round her ankles. Her toes bulged through the satin. 'You'd better take it off,' said Susan, 'your feet are too fat.'

'Come on,' said Gillian, 'I'll show you.' She smiled as she arranged Sharon's hands and feet. But when her feet were right, her arms flapped as she tried to balance. When her arms were right, she toppled forward.

'You'd be all right if you came to lessons,' Gillian said. 'Sorry, I forgot. Your mum can't afford it.' She smothered a giggle. Susan held her arms out awkwardly and fell over her own feet, then collapsed laughing on the bed. Gillian gave Susan a warning look. 'Don't worry,' she said to Sharon, 'not everyone's good at dancing.'

Sharon's face grew hot. She wanted to slap Susan, to pinch her hard, to pull her hair. 'I'm going to ask your mum for some squash. Anyone else want some?' Neither girl replied. They spun around so that the chiffon scarves tied around their waists whipped like kite tails.

As Sharon passed the living room door, she saw Gillian's mum staring into the fire and sipping from a tall, thin glass. She was crying, rocking backwards and forwards. Sharon had seen her own mum cry once. Grown-ups liked to pretend that they weren't upset when kids were around. It would be best not to ask for the drink, just to get it. She took three tumblers off the kitchen draining board and tipped some squash into each from the jug on the table. In between the sound of the sobs from the living room, she could hear the thuds of the dancing girls in the room above. If she could just find something to poison Susan's squash, then she would have Gillian to herself. The Fairy Liquid, or the Vim by the kitchen sink: either of them might work.

She sat on a stool sipping her drink, and looking up to the Russian dolls on the shelf. Gillian didn't care about them any more than she cared about Sharon. She climbed on the stool and reached up, holding the wooden dolls as carefully as if they were made of china. She twisted the middle of each doll, and lined them up in height order on the table, five of them, like the children in her family: Kieran, then Maggie; Sharon, then Brendan, and, last of all, little Janice who, try as she might, would not twist open.

The sound of a key in the front door made her jump. She tried to open the largest doll to place the next one inside, but the join in the middle was stiff. She opened the next doll, but the smallest one would have to go in the next smallest one first and then into the middle one. There were half bodies all over the table as the shape of Gillian's dad appeared in the glass panel of the front door. He was opening and shutting an umbrella in the porch. She pushed the kitchen door closed with her foot, but it didn't shut all the way. She grabbed her schoolbag and scooped the dolls, halves and wholes, into it. 'For God's sake, Anne, pull yourself together.' Gillian's dad spoke in a loud whisper, like when Sharon's mum told her dad off, late at night, when he came in from the pub. The crying became louder along with a sound like a smack, then a whimper, like when the dog got under her mum's feet.

Sharon crept through the hall. Trembling, she buckled her shoes and reached for her coat, clutching her schoolbag in the other hand. The living room door opened. 'Hello, ginger nut.' Gillian's dad smiled and rubbed her head. She flinched. His smile faded.

'I'm not feeling well. Can I go home, please?' As she slipped her arm into the sleeve of her mac she dropped her bag, and the dolls tumbled onto the floor.

'Well, well, well,' he said, 'look what ginger nut's been up to, Anne.' Gillian's mum stood beside him, her hand covering her cheek. He guided Sharon into the living room, pressing on her shoulder to make her sit on the sofa. 'Would you like to explain yourself, young lady?' Sharon clasped her hands together, to stop them shaking. She swallowed hard. 'Cat got your tongue?' he asked.

'Can't you see she's frightened, Alan?' Gillian's mum said.

'I was only playing,' Sharon said, 'I couldn't get them back together, so...'

'So you thought you'd steal them.' Gillian's dad stood over her, his face leaning down towards hers.

'No, I heard crying, and ...'

His face changed. 'Go to the kitchen while I decide what to do with you. Get out of my sight.'

She sat at the table watching the second hand of the clock click round. What would her mum say when she found out? There'd be no party to go to, no anything. Perhaps if she went to confession she could wipe it out and start again. She could hear Gillian's dad in the living room; his voice sounded angry and hard. Gillian's mum spoke softly, interrupting him as he spoke. They both came into the kitchen, and Gillian's dad said, 'We'll let it pass this time. No need to talk about what's happened here. No need at all. Do you understand?'

Back home, Vince the postman was asking Diane to go for a drink in the bar of the Crossroads Motel. 'Where's Mum?' Sharon said.

'Upstairs. Dad's home; left work early because of the rain.' Maggie said.

Sharon walked upstairs, placing both feet on each step before going on to the next. Her heart was beating fast. She stopped on the last step but one. There were voices in her mum and dad's room. Her dad passed her on the stairs, his eyes fixed on something far away. 'Hi, Dad,' she said. He didn't speak, just rubbed her head. Sharon reached into her bag for the party invitation and found the smallest doll nestling at the bottom. She turned it over in her hand. The baby, like Janice. She knocked on the bedroom door; her mother was sitting on the side of the bed, winding a rolled-up hankie in and out of her fingers.

'Yes, love.'

'I'm invited to Gillian's party. Can I have a new dress, please?' Sharon showed her the invitation.

Her mum sighed. 'We'll see what we can do.'

Maggie and Sharon were tidying the bedroom: dusting whilst dancing to the Noel Edmonds show on Maggie's transistor with knickers on their heads and socks on their hands, clean clothes that they were supposed to be putting away. They pursed their lips to hold in the giggles until they spurted out in a spray of spit. 'Stop playing the eejit and get on with it,' their mum shouted up the stairs.

'Mum's got to go into hospital,' Maggie said.

'What's wrong with her? She's not dying, is she?'

'No, stupid, it's just some tests. Mum says it's nothing

to worry about.' Maggie pushed the Ewbank under Sharon's bed. It hit against the shoebox. 'What do you keep in there, locks of Gillian's hair?'

Sharon blushed. 'Leave it, it's mine.' Maggie tipped the shoebox onto the bed: bubble gum cards, seashells and stones, a hair ribbon, a handkerchief and the smallest of Gillian's dolls.

'You and Gillian, are you like lesbe friends?' Maggie wriggled her hips and pushed out her chest. She dangled the handkerchief before Sharon's nose. 'Come on, Sharon, it's Gillian this, Gillian that, Gillian's perfect house, perfect mum and dad who give her everything.'

'They're not perfect; they're horrible. I never want to see them again.' Tears pricked at Sharon's eyes.

'But you've been going on about this party...' Maggie stood back as Sharon reached for the nail scissors on the dressing table, and cut at the handkerchief and ribbon. She tried sawing at the middle of the doll with the open blade of the scissors. It left no more than a scratch on the red paint.

'Hey!' Maggie prised the scissors from her fingers. 'Are you going to tell me what's going on?'

'I'll take Sharon to the party,' Maggie said.

'Thanks, love.' Their mum lowered herself into the armchair. She hadn't been up to much since she'd come home from hospital after those tests. She'd even missed Mass on Sunday, and she'd forgotten about the new dress. Sharon was wearing a hand-me-down from her cousin. Susan had been boasting about her new dress all week. It was bound to be embroidered with real gold thread. And she had moved to the desk next to Gillian's, leaving Sharon paired up with Peter O'Doherty.

Maggie had a date with Simon whilst the party was on. She breathed on her cupped hand, sniffed it, and unwrapped a stick of Wrigley's Spearmint gum. She offered one to Sharon, but she bit her lip and shook her head. 'Why are you making me go?' she said as they reached the top of Gillian's road.

'You're not going to the party. Do you think I'd let you near that creep?'

They stopped at the house next door to Gillian's. 'Wait here.' Sharon stooped behind the hedge holding the card and the wrapped present, a French knitting set. Inside Gillian's house it was bright with balloons and noise. The hem of Sharon's petticoat scratched against her knees and the wind whipped at the skin between her dress and the top of her socks.

'Which one's his car?' Maggie said. Sharon pointed at a pale blue Cortina parked a few yards up the kerb. Maggie pulled a long two-pronged fork from her bag, the one their mother used to stick in joints of meat as she carved them. She crouched on the pavement by the side of the car. 'You keep a look out,' she said as she speared the tyres, front and back.

The lights went down in Gillian's house as the candles were lit on the cake. 'Give me the card and present,' Maggie said. 'Now stay out of sight.' Gillian's dad opened the door. 'Hello, I'm Sharon's sister. I'm afraid she's not well, but she wanted Gillian to have this.'

'How sweet. Won't you come in?'

'No, thank you, but could I have a piece of cake to take home and a party bag for Sharon?'

Maggie handed Sharon a small plastic bag and a piece of cake wrapped in a serviette. 'There's your evidence. You've been to the party, okay?' Sharon nodded, her mouth hanging open. 'Hurry up; we're meeting Simon at the Wimpy Bar.'

'What shall I do with this?' Sharon held out the small doll. She had hoped to put it back when no-one was looking.

Maggie shrugged. 'Burn it, bin it. You don't want anything from them.' She grabbed Sharon's hand. Sharon turned the doll over in her pocket as they ran for the bus.

Ruined

Graham sauntered over and drew Maggie close as the opening bars of 'Lonely Girl' blared from the speakers. 'That's you next week,' he said as they danced round and round, his hands resting just above her knicker-line.

'Mmm?' She raised her head from his shoulder. He looked a bit like David Cassidy from that angle. The ultraviolet light picked out a white thread on his dark shirt.

'Lonely Girl, that's you next week.'

'Mmm.' She narrowed her eyes in what she hoped was a sexy way, and parted her lips. They kissed throughout the song, and then the lights came on. It was the moment she hated, like at the Odeon when the magic of the film turned into an emptying room littered with dog-ends and plastic cups.

She zipped her satin bomber jacket to just below her

cleavage and slid her fingers along her shoulder blades to ease her bra straps straight. She checked her hair and make-up in the flower-shaped mirror she kept in her handbag, and waited for Graham to say goodbye to his mates. He grabbed her hand, and they headed out into the high street, stopping to kiss in the doorway of Burton's, then Woolworth's, then on to Maggie's road.

They lingered on the path outside her house, lit by the flicker of the TV through the gap in the living room curtains. 'I'll write to you,' she said, licking the last drops of his saliva from her bottom lip. He slipped his hands beneath her T-shirt and was working with one hand behind her back to unclip her bra, which she had refastened several times on the walk home. He rubbed her breast with the other hand and groaned; his face contorted. She felt her nipples harden and a sudden wetness in her knickers. 'Best not,' she said. She pecked him gently on the forehead. He pulled down the scoop neck of her top and sucked hard at a spot above the lace of her bra. She pushed his head away, and then drew him in for one last kiss. She felt a hardening against her thigh. He pulled her hand towards the zip of his jeans.

She had read a book where the heroine suggested going for a hamburger whenever a boy got too persistent. But the book was set in America where there were burger bars on every corner, and a girl's worth was measured in how many cashmere sweaters she owned. It wouldn't work in England; they were miles from the Wimpy bar, and she got most of her clothes from the market. Besides, there were only so many burgers you could eat in one evening. She wriggled her hand free.

'Okay, I get the message.' He held his hands up in surrender, gave her a peck on the lips. 'See you when you get back from Ireland.'

Her dad was waiting in the hall as she came in. She

wondered how much he had seen through the glass panel of the front door. Her skin would now be puckering and red. She felt it glowing like a beacon through the fabric of her top. She kept her jacket on, shivering as if she were cold. 'Was that the quare fella?' he said.

'His name is Graham, Dad. And you want to watch how you use that word around English people.' She could smell whiskey on his breath.

'Ah, the quare fella covers it well enough. Graham, the quare fella, this week, another quare fella next week.'

'Will you come and sit on this suitcase, Maggie?' Her mother's head emerged above a pile of ironing in the living room.

Maggie sighed. 'What's the point of ironing everything when you'll iron it again at the other end?'

'Don't be so bold. What would the customs men be thinking if they opened our cases?' She was cramming a pair of men's shoes into the last available space.

'Dad's shoes? Dad isn't even coming.'

'They're for your Uncle Thomas. And there are bits in there for Chrissie too.'

'Don't they have shoe shops in Ireland?'

Her dad gave her that *don't push it with your mother* look. 'Put the kettle on, Maggie.' He followed her into the kitchen and put four slices of Mother's Pride under the grill. 'Now, you'll help your mother out while you're away, won't you? You and Sharon are big enough to help out with Brendan and Janice. Don't leave her with everything to do.'

'Of course.' But she didn't meet his eye as she busied herself with knives, plates, butter and jam.

'Kieran and me, well we'll cope as long as there's rashers and eggs.'

She started a letter to Graham on the train from Euston to

Holyhead, writing in green ink on long sheets of peach-tinted paper that she had folded to fit into her handbag. She headed it: *Monday, on the train.* She woke with a jolt, her arm on the table in front of her covering the only additional words, *Dear Graham.*

Her mum was handing out sandwiches from two Waitrose carrier bags. She wiped Janice's fingers before she had finished her last mouthful. Janice dipped them into a bag of crisps and crammed half the packet into her mouth. 'God, grant me patience.' Janice squirmed as her mum rubbed her face with a damp flannel. 'Maggie, will you take Brendan to the toilet.'

'Can't Sharon...?' she began, but Sharon was asleep, her head lolling on her folded arms on the table in front of her. Maggie refolded the letter to Graham, placed it in her bag, and began the swaying trek to the nearest toilet.

Everything was in miniature in Lahinch: a mini fairground, a tiny cinema. Their caravan was small – one of the pod ones where you had to pull the beds out at night – and when one person turned in their sleep, the whole caravan rocked.

'Can we ask Auntie Chrissie if we can stay with her, Mum?' Maggie said as they were folding the beds back into the benches in the morning, 'Just me and Sharon?' Their mother had spent several minutes fiddling with the Calor Gas stove to light the flame beneath the kettle. There was a growing pile of spent matches to the side of it, and a heady smell that made Maggie feel drunk.

'And why would your great aunt be wanting a couple of young girls in the house at her time of life?' She set out two bowls on the worktop next to the cooker and stood with another three stacked in her left hand, all usable space exhausted. She passed four bowls to Maggie, a box of cornflakes to Sharon, a bottle of milk to Brendan and five spoons to Janice. 'Thank God Kieran and your father aren't here,' their mother said, 'we'd be putting them outside on deckchairs.'

'It's a bit damp for that,' said Sharon, nodding towards the rain beating at the windowpanes. The caravan was rocking in the wind.

'Just think, Mum, if we were at Aunt Chrissie's you could have a bed to yourself,' Maggie said. Sharon mouthed 'Good one, Maggie'.

'Ah, you're all heart, aren't you? No thought for yourselves at all.'

'And we'll be back to help with Brendan and Janice,' Maggie added.

'I know your kind of help.'

'Can we at least ask? See what Auntie Chrissie has to say?'

Their mother gave a deep sigh. 'Okay, we'll take a walk to Ennistymon. But I'm not promising anything.'

Auntie Chrissie was wearing a floral crossover pinafore. Her boobs hung beneath it like two beach balls with the air let out. Wispy tendrils escaped from her hair, which was scraped back into a tight bun. With the light behind her, it looked like she had a halo. 'Jaysus, lads, you've brought the weather with you.' She herded them into the sitting room, admiring each child in turn. 'Will you look at the size of you,' she said, 'and you could do with a cup of tea.' She guided Maggie's mum to the armchair.

'Ah, they've done nothing but moan since we left the caravan. You'd think they'd never had to walk in the rain in their lives.'

'They've a soft life in England, God love 'em.'

A picture hung above the table, Jesus with his chest torn open, his heart dripping blood. Next to this was a brown-tinted photo of a nun. Janice picked up a statue of

Our Lady from the sideboard and, tipping it from one side to another, walked it across to a wooden crucifix adorned with a white plastic Jesus in a loincloth. The loincloth troubled Maggie. What was beneath? Did it work like other men's willies, or was he smooth like Brendan's Action Man?

'Will you leave me bit of religion alone?' Aunt Chrissie said. 'Go and look at the donkeys in the field out the back. You can see them through the kitchen window.' She ushered Brendan and Janice to look at two sodden donkeys hanging their heads in the driving rain. 'Ah, if only I'd been blessed with grandchildren. But Carmel was called,' she gestured towards the photo of the nun, 'and my Thomas, well...'

The door slammed, and there were heavy footsteps in the hall. 'Have you taken your wellies off, Thomas?' There were grunts as the steps backtracked. Uncle Thomas stood in the doorway of the sitting room in mud-splattered trousers and thick socks, the colour of porridge. He smelt of cows and rain. Maggie was unsure how to look at him. One of his eyes stared ahead, coated in a milky glaze as the other moved about the room. He nodded and muttered something unintelligible.

Maggie's mother set about making the tea. 'It's a bit crowded in the caravan, Auntie Chrissie. We were wondering if Maggie and Sharon could stay with you.'

'God love 'em, Maura, I'd have them to live.' She rubbed her hands together. 'They'll be wanting to go to the dance tomorrow night. Thomas can meet them after, walk them home.'

Posters for *The Dancehall Sweethearts*, the latest album by The Horslips, who were playing that night, were plastered to the doors of the dancehall. Everyone was jigging about from the first number – laughing, singing and shouting at each other. Maggie and Sharon squeezed through the crowd and found a place to stand not far from the stage. The singer's trousers were so tight; Maggie found it hard to bring her eyes up to his face. She was going to nudge Sharon, point it out, but then Sharon was too young to notice such things.

A tall, skinny boy was dancing near to her, his cork-screw hair flying. When the rhythm slowed, he veered towards Maggie, lifted her by the waist and put her down a few feet away. 'What do you think you're doing?' she said. Her face was reddening. She could feel the pressure of his fingers on her waist.

'I wanted to see if you were stuck. You haven't moved all evening.' He leaned in close to her ear as he spoke. She could feel his breath on her neck.

'Maybe some of us don't want to throw ourselves around like lunatics,' she said. She felt that she should move away, but she could feel her body inclining towards his shoulder. He smelt of sweat, and there were widening dark circles under the arms of his T-shirt. It had seen better days, as had his jeans, which had a frayed hole on the left knee.

'So, are you dancing, or not?'

'Um, I'm looking after my little sister.' But as she turned to where Sharon had been standing, she wasn't there, only her Chelsea Girl bag, beige suede with the brown appliquéd butterfly, propped up against her own bag on the floor.

'Is that her over there?' He gestured towards a group of girls and boys at the back of the hall. Sharon was with them, sipping Coke through a straw. 'Looks like you're free then, Blondie.'

'Maggie, Margaret.'

'Ah, you're Maura's girl, staying at Chrissie Coughlan's.'

'How do you know?'

'I have my sources.' He drew his back straight and tapped the side of his nose. 'Come on, so, I'll get you a drink. I'm Declan, Declan O'Halloran.' After a few nervous glances across to Sharon, she deposited her sister's handbag on her shoulder and left her to her new friends.

Declan's eyes would not stay still, darting constantly, and his body twitched, like the music was a part of him. He was drinking cider, which she could smell on his breath. It was hard to hear what he said with the music pumping out. It meant pressing his mouth close to her ear, and even then she could barely hear him, just feel his breath on her face, his hand on her shoulder.

He grabbed her hand as the band finished, and led her to the door. 'I'll see you outside in a bit,' Maggie said to Sharon as they passed her on the way out. Sharon was deep in conversation with a ginger-haired boy. Maggie's fingers tingled at the feel of Declan's hand in hers. She thought of Graham back in England. This didn't count, did it? She was on holiday. No-one would know.

She was kissing Declan as Uncle Thomas arrived to walk them up the unlit road to Ennistymon. He nodded and grunted at Declan. Maggie blushed, and excused herself to go and find Sharon, leaving Declan and Uncle Thomas together. Uncle Thomas said very little to them on the walk home, just cleared his throat a few times and muttered. Sometimes the muttering rose in tone, like he might be asking a question. Maggie hoped she was nodding in the right places.

When she went to bed, she draped a scarf over the crucifix on the dressing table. She didn't want Jesus watching over her as she slept, or as her fingers wandered below her nightie as she remembered Declan's tongue in her mouth.

'Ah, Declan O'Halloran, you could do worse,' Aunt Chrissie said over breakfast the next morning. 'He'll be coming into some land soon enough. And he's a good worker.'

'It's not his prospects she's interested in,' Sharon said, giggling.

Maggie cast her a piercing look. 'I've got a boyfriend back home, Auntie Chrissie. His name's Graham.'

'Now what would you be wanting with an English boy? Declan, he'd give you babies.'

'Babies!'

'You have to think about these things early on. Yes, lots of babies.'

Sharon spat her tea back into the cup whilst Maggie made 'rescue me' signs with her eyes. Maggie started clearing the table.

'Ach, no, away with ye. You don't want to be doing the washing-up on your holidays. You'll be off to look at the boys on the beach. Don't keep them waiting.'

Maggie and Sharon arrived in Lahinch with their rolled-up towels tucked under their arms. Brendan and Janice were playing outside the caravan with a blow-up beach ball, which kept being blown away by the wind. Through the doorway, they could see their mother standing at the cooker. The pile of spent matches was growing into an unruly pyramid. She breathed a sigh as the two girls entered the caravan. 'Honest to God, I'm sick to death of this cooker.' A flame caught beneath the kettle and she looked for a clean cup, but the small round washing-up bowl was full of dirty dishes. 'I need the hot water to wash the cups, but if I wash the cups there'll be no water left for a coffee.' She looked for a moment as though she might explode, then she threw her arms into the air. 'Come on now, girls, go and fetch some water.'

'Mum, we're on holiday,' Maggie said.

'Holiday, is it? Where's the holiday for me? You two swanning off to Chrissie's and leaving me with the little ones.'

'You said we could!' said Sharon.

'Knowing there'd be moaning if I didn't.'

Maggie breathed out heavily. 'Leave it, Mum, we'll do the washing-up later.'

'Will you now? I don't believe it for a minute.' She scuttled off with the washing-up bowl towards the standpipe at the other end of the field.

Janice insisted on bringing the ball to the beach, even though it was too big to get her arms around and had to be fetched by Sharon each time it broke away. 'Ah, she'll get bored of it soon enough,' their mother said.

'I'll get bored of it before she does,' Sharon said.

'Will you ever stop moaning? She's only little…'

'You have to make allowances,' Maggie and Sharon chanted together.

There were a couple of teenage boys braving the waves, posing in their trunks and trying not to huddle their shoulders against the chill. Maggie and Sharon uncovered their goose-pimpled flesh as the younger ones wriggled into their costumes beneath their towels.

'What's that mark?'

Maggie pulled at the strap of her bikini and avoided her mother's eyes.

'Sharon, take the little ones down to the water.'

'But, Mum.'

'Don't argue.'

Janice and Brendan chased the ball along the beach until Brendan caught up with it and kicked it into the sea.

'I know what that mark means.' She spoke through the narrowest gap between her lips, each word given the same quiet emphasis.

'It doesn't mean anything,' Maggie said, pulling her T-shirt back over her head.

'You only get those if you've…' She paused, then, in a breathy whisper, '…gone all the way.'

Maggie laughed.

'Don't be so bold. I didn't get five children without knowing a thing or two.'

Maggie pictured her mum with a big pregnant belly and a necklace of love bites. She went to bed with so many clothes on – full set of underwear, neck-to-toe flannelette nightie – maybe her neck was the only place her dad could reach. 'Look, Mum, Graham and I haven't…'

'But one thing can lead to another and, before you know it, you're ruined.' She shook out a large towel and spread it on the sand, the wind catching beneath it so it arched like a caterpillar.

Sharon ran up the beach and dropped onto the towel, drawing the sides up to rub her legs. She looked from Maggie to her mother and, as if to fill the silence, she said, 'I made some new friends last night, Mum.'

'Friends, is it? Nice friends, I hope. And was your sister looking after you?' She gave Maggie a sideways glance.

'She was looking after someone else,' she giggled. 'What's his name? Declan, isn't it?' Maggie winced like a dog waiting to be kicked. Her mother breathed in sharply through the nose.

'And what about Graham?'

Maggie shrugged. 'Graham's back home in Epsom.'

'I see; Graham putting his mark on you has made no difference to your morals, then.' She looked at Maggie like she looked at her dad when he came home drunk.

'You've got to play the field, Mum,' said Sharon.

'Hah! Is that what they tell you in that comic you read?'

'Magazine, Mum. *Jackie* is a magazine.'

Two lads in skimpy swimming-trunks came bounding up with the beach ball. 'Are you after losing this?' the taller one said to Sharon.

'Oh yes, thanks.' She was sitting with her arms propped behind her, sticking out her chest.

'Do you fancy a swim?' he said, his eyes fixed on Sharon's bikini top. Sharon ignored the T-shirt that her mother offered her, and ran towards the water.

'You're gorgeous, you know that?' Declan whispered as he stroked Maggie's hair, his arm draped over the back of the cinema seat. He smelt of the turf he had been digging all day. As they kissed, she tried to tune into the soundtrack of the film – Goldie Hawn, Warren Beatty, bank robbery – she memorised a few lines of dialogue. 'Am I keeping you from the film?' He pronounced it *fillum*.

'No, but Mum will ask about it. I don't want her to think...'

'Never mind your mammy.' He kissed her until she thought she would never breathe again. As she surfaced, she saw Sharon and her new friend Terence two rows in front. Terence edged his arm along Sharon's shoulder and slid his hand down her front.

That night, Maggie wrote to Graham: 'Went to a dance, went to a film and went to the beach.' No mention of Declan. What Father Westland would call a sin of omission. The next morning, she dropped by the Post Office for a stamp and chose a postcard with a map of Ireland. It reminded her of a smiling old man with wild hair and a ragged beard. She made a cross on the old man's beard before she put it in the envelope, put another cross on the back of the card and wrote, 'We are here'.

Uncle Thomas had walked Maggie and Sharon home from the cinema and passed on to his mother all that he'd seen with his one good eye. 'Terence O'Connor,' Aunt Chrissie said to Sharon, 'and the both of you with your fine red hair. Think of it, you could have ginger twins. There's twins on the Coughlan side – and your babies would be bound to be ginger.'

At the Saturday dance, Maggie abandoned herself to the music, alive to Declan's touch. Sharon was at the back of the hall, jigging around with Terence, in a competition to see whose hair was the fieriest. 'Ginger twins,' Maggie said. She laughed so much that she couldn't tell Declan the joke.

Declan passed her an oblong box. Inside was a silver pendant with her star sign, Gemini. 'You can wear it till the next time you're over.' He stood close behind her and fastened it at the back of her neck, pushing her hair to one side and stooping to kiss her shoulder. He slipped his arms around her waist, entwining his fingers with hers on the waistband of her satin flares, his chin resting on the bare flesh above the scoop of her T-shirt as they swayed to the music. He stroked her stomach, his fingernails catching on the satin, and she leaned back to kiss him.

Maggie was floating as he led her from the dancehall down to the beach. The night was still and warm. Her wide trousers billowed as she walked. The satin stroked her thighs and slapped against her shins. She could hear the rhythms from the dancehall, then whooping and hollering from O'Brien's bar, and then the only sound was the crashing of the waves on the rocks beyond the bay. That's how it was in the old films, the ones that her mum liked to watch on a Saturday afternoon: man, woman, neck arched in ecstasy, then waves crashing on rocks.

She rested her hand on his back, inside the hem of his T-shirt so she could feel his skin. He turned and pulled her close, and kissed her hard so the stubble on his chin scratched her lip. She wanted to pull away and draw closer at the same time. His hands edged upwards, pushing her top higher up her back, his callused palms dragging on the fabric. She tried to block him with her elbows. 'You know I'm falling for you, Blondie,' he said.

'Take it slow, eh?'

'Come on now, you're away home soon.' His prick was hard against her as he licked and bit her neck.

'Don't mark me, please.' Her voice sounded faint, as if it didn't belong to her. His hands forceful now, he unclipped her bra and buried his head beneath her top, his curls spread across her breasts. She shuddered. He unhooked the top button of her trousers and worked the zip down. He tore it free as it snagged on the satin. She thought about saying that she had her period, but his fingers were inside her knickers before she could speak, rubbing hard on her clitoris. The kisses alone had made her as wet as when she touched herself beneath the bedclothes at night, and now she came quickly.

He pushed his fingers further, harder, inside her now. It hurt and she tried to wriggle free. He lowered her down to the sand, blistered fists of seaweed surrounding her head like mermaids' hair. He grabbed her hand and pulled it towards his unzipped jeans. His underpants were nylon, the fabric pilled, her fingers below the snap of the waistband now, his hand firm on her wrist, his hand over hers, sliding up and down, his face twisted.

She closed her eyes; she didn't want to see. She wanted to rewind to the scene in the dancehall, his arms around her, him fastening the pendant round her neck. The waves crashed on the rocks beyond the bay.

Cold Salt Water

He comes in, with his shirt splattered with blood, and I say, 'Honest to God, Kieran.'

'Don't fuss, Mum,' he says like it's nothing to walk in the house with your nose spread across your face.

'What in Jesus' name happened?' No answer. 'Who were you with?'

'John and Chris.'

'And are they hurt too?'

'Leave it, Mum.'

I put my hand up to his face, but he dips from it. 'It's a rough old place, that dancehall. Tiffany's was it?'

'It's a disco, Mum, not a dancehall.'

And then his father's in the doorway, and I say, 'Will you look at the state of Kieran?' But he's three sheets to the wind himself, so I send him off to bed.

Well, I try to whip the shirt off the boy, but he holds it

close around him. So I get a bucket ready: cold water with a good dash of salt. 'Come on now, Kieran,' I say, 'Let's have that shirt.' It's one of his good ones, a Ben Sherman. He unbuttons it. There are bruises like footprints on his chest.

'Did you get a look at them? Could you describe them to the police?'

'Please, Mum. It doesn't matter.'

'You've bruises all over!'

He flinches as I touch him. I can see that he's trying to hold on to the tears. I know the wobble in that lip, like when his father used to tell him that boys don't cry, so he'd sniff the snot back up into his nose, and pretend he was all right. But a mother knows. But a mother only knows by rummaging in his chest of drawers when he's out, through the piles of pennies and silver in the top drawer from his turned out pockets. I go in there when I'm short of money for the milkman or need a 50p when the electric's gone. He doesn't like the rattle of the coins in his pockets and how they spoil the line of his trousers. So they pyramid higher in the drawer, silver on copper, and slip like the coal in the bunker as the drawer opens, heavier each time I pull it out. And that's where I found that thing once, from a packet of three as they call it, and only the one left. I told him what Father Westland would say. He just laughed. Though there have been times when I've thought, wouldn't we have been glad of one?

He's been worse since he's been working, acting like he's man of the house. Home at six, he slams the back door open against the kitchen dresser – there's a hole in the hardboard now – then he shouts, 'Where's my dinner?' When he was small, I could slap him across the back of the legs, but now he stands above me. I need to stand on a chair to look him in the eye.

'I'm off to bed,' Kieran says. I watch as he climbs the

stairs, every step an effort. Whether he sleeps or not, I don't know, but I lie awake next to his snoring father. Every time I close my eyes, I can't stop seeing the footprints on my boy's chest.

In the morning, he's so stiff he can hardly raise an arm, so I knock at Mick Bennett's house and ask would he tell them at the factory that Kieran won't be in. Then I run Kieran a hot bath to see would it ease him a little, and make him egg and bacon when he's out and dressed. Although it hurts to see him like that, it's nice, in a way, to have my boy to myself, with Jack and the children off for the day.

I've the radio on in the kitchen, and the news headlines come over, of the latest from the IRA, a pub in Guildford, not ten miles up the road. I know there'll be hard stares when I ask for the veg at the greengrocer, when I open my mouth to speak, as if it was me that laid that bomb. 'Are you ready to tell me?' I say, as he wipes the yolk of his egg off the plate with a half-bitten slice of fried bread. He holds up his mug, and I pour some more tea. 'Shall we go to the police?' He half-drains the mug, then slams it down on the table. The tea splashes up the sides then settles again. 'Or was it you that started it? I know your temper.'

The full story of the bombing comes on the radio. 'Switch it off,' he says.

'God knows why your father stands up for that lot,' I say, 'it doesn't do us any good, those of us that have to live here.' He stares at his plate, his fingertips pressing into the edge of the table. 'Is that what the fight was over?' I say.

'It's nothing to do with me, what the Irish get up to,' he says. 'I ain't Irish.'

I wipe my hands on a tea towel and turn to him. 'Only every ounce of blood that flows through your veins.'

'It don't make me Irish.' He butters a slice of bread. I can see how it's bothering him to eat, with his top lip split. Part of me wants to slap him and the rest of me wants to cradle him. I picture him lying on the ground as the heavy boots hit his chest. And I think of how he's stopped going to the Tara club, how it's Tiffany's on a Saturday night, out with his packet of three: Durex, approved to British standards.

I go to the bucket where I'd steeped the shirt the night before. The water is pink, the blood seeping into the crystals. I drain the bucket into the sink, rinse the shirt, then run more cold water into the bucket, emptying the remainder of the packet of Saxa into it. I watch the shirt sink, pushing it down so it's covered.

Saturday Girl

Sharon couldn't write *Get well soon* in the card that was passed around at tea break; Lou wasn't going to get better. She thought of putting something about there not being so many breakages on sweets without Lou there; they were allowed to buy the broken bars of chocolate cheap, and Lou would drop whatever she fancied on the floor. But Sharon didn't want to let Mrs Harris know that they were doing it, so she just wrote *luv Sharon* in the card, and dropped a 50p piece into the collection.

Mrs Harris had gathered the Saturday staff on the shop floor that morning, before opening time, and told them that Lou had leukaemia. They were to hope for the best, but prepare for bad news. She said to stay cheerful, for Lou's sake, as she wouldn't want them to be sad, and that work was a good distraction, so carry on as normal.

Steve chose the present for Lou, a transistor radio off records and electrical. He gave it to her that evening, at visiting time. He said they only had hospital radio on the headphones by the bed, so it was a good gift. It meant that Lou could listen to the Sunday record charts on Radio 1.

Steve wore segs on his shoes – metal quarter-moons that you battered into your heels when they were wearing down. They clicked on the hard floor in Woolworth's as he paced around looking for things to supervise. They had both fancied him, Sharon and Lou, but then there was the Queen's Silver Jubilee party at the football club. Sharon and Lou had pogoed to the Sex Pistols with Ralph, then bopped to 'Hound Dog' with Paul, but when it came to a slow song, Steve danced with Lou. She spent the rest of the evening sitting on Steve's lap, snogging.

The next Saturday, Mrs Harris gathered them all again and told them that Lou had died the day before; *passed away quietly in her sleep* were her actual words. They delayed the opening of the shop for a few minutes as Lou's friends took in the news. Then Mrs Harris said that they must get on with their work; that it was better to carry on with your day when you've had a shock, rather than sit brooding. Sharon dried her tears, and took her place behind the sweet counter. There was sniffling all day, and girls asking permission to leave the shop floor, which wasn't usually allowed outside of break-times, but Mrs Harris was kinder than usual. Sharon tried not to think of Lou all the time, but whenever she placed a broken chocolate bar in the box beneath the counter, her eyes filled. It wasn't helped by Ralph, who was on records, playing 'Seasons in the Sun' over and over, until Mrs Harris gently took the record off the turntable. "Goodbye to you, my trusted friend," sung over and over, was more than anyone could stand.

Lou would only have got to hear the charts once while she was in hospital, the day after Steve brought in the radio. Sharon wondered what had happened to it.

Steve's segs clattered as they followed the coffin into the crematorium. All the Saturday girls sat together, and Steve was on the aisle next to Sharon. He was wearing the suit he wore to work, black with a pinstripe. There was dandruff on the shoulders.

It was different from other funerals that Sharon had been to. When the old nun died, who had taught at the Convent of the Sacred Heart, the service had been long and boring and in Latin. Some of the older girls had seen Sister Mary Patrick in her coffin, been forced to file past, and there had been giggling afterwards and tales from those who claimed to have kissed her dead lips, her cold forehead. Sharon had been spared that, being in the first year at the time. And the girls hadn't gone to the graveside; just the Kyrie and all that in the convent chapel. Sharon had got through it by thinking that *Magpie* would be on telly later. She had a crush on Mick, the one with the long hair. She'd put the words of the *Magpie* theme tune to the tunes of the Latin hymns, sung them softly. They went quite well. But this service, in the crematorium, was more in-your-face. As the coffin rolled through the heavy curtains, Sharon looked up from her fistful of soggy tissues to see tears glistening on Steve's cheeks.

The Woolworth's girls weren't invited back to Lou's house – only family and close friends, and they seemed to be friends of Lou's mum and dad rather than anyone she had hung around with. Steve was asked back to the house, but he said he had to get back to work, though Sharon had heard Mrs Harris tell him to take the whole day off.

He didn't speak as they waited for the bus, but when the 406 arrived and it came to buying tickets, he said 'I'll get these' as Sharon fumbled in her bag for her purse. He dipped a hand in his trouser pocket, pulled out a palmful of change, and picked out some coins with his other hand. 'Let's go upstairs.' He held onto the metal pole at the bottom of the stairs, and waited for her to go up first. She would have liked to sit at the front, but didn't want to appear childish, so she chose the long seat at the back.

'I couldn't go back to the house,' he said. 'Lou's mum and dad, they kept introducing me to all these people – Lou's aunts and uncles and that – as Lou's boyfriend.'

'Too much?'

'Too much.' He pulled a pack of Juicy Fruit out of his jacket pocket and pushed a stick towards her with his thumb, like he was offering a cigarette. She shook her head. She'd had to give up chewing gum since having her brace fitted. 'It's not as though we went out for long.'

'No.' She wasn't sure whether she needed to say anything, but that one word felt okay. She ran her tongue round the metal on her top teeth. She was glad that smiling wasn't required; Lou had had a perfect smile, without the aid of an orthodontist. Sharon had thought her to be lucky, before the leukaemia.

'Awful, though – one week you're out dancing with your girlfriend and the next you're visiting her in hospital.'

'And then you're going to her funeral.'

They fell silent. The bus came to a halt and the top deck emptied of passengers. Sharon placed a hand on Steve's arm. She'd seen her mum do it to Mrs Hubbard next door, after Mr Hubbard died. Steve attempted a smile. 'You're a good kid, Sharon.' She didn't like 'kid', but she liked his fingers squeezing hers as he held her hand. She edged closer to him.

Katrina joined Sharon on the sweet counter the Saturday after the funeral. She was the kind of girl Sharon's mum didn't approve of, with thick mascara and big gold jewellery. She didn't pull her weight like Lou had done; she only looked busy when a supervisor passed by. And she was a bit dim. She'd been on fruit and veg before, which was next to the sweet counter, and when she was told to straighten up the bananas, she'd stood there trying to get the bend out of a bunch of them. Lou and Sharon had had a good laugh about that. Sharon saw Katrina bend down beneath the counter and slip fifty-pence pieces into her bra after serving customers. She did it several times that first morning on sweets.

Sharon planned to go to Dorothy Perkins at lunchtime. There was a brown skirt and a cream top, with a little brown collar to match the skirt, which she'd tried on a few weeks before when she didn't have quite enough cash. Lou had told her about the outfit, said it would suit her colouring. Lou was good at that sort of thing; she could walk into a shop and pick out clothes in seconds.

Sharon was ripping the top off her pay packet when Paul caught up with her outside the glass doors of Woolworth's. He pulled a comb out of his back pocket and adjusted his quiff. 'All right, gorgeous?' he said. He was wearing a leather jacket in spite of the warmth of the sun.

'So, is it *Happy Days,* that look?'

He stopped short, hand to his chest as if he'd been stabbed. 'Elvis was King long before the Fonz came to our screens.' She smiled. Clothes were like badges to tell people who you were: her sister Maggie with her long hippy skirts; Ralph with his safety pins and bondage trousers; Paul in his brothel creepers and drape jackets; the greasers that gathered by the hot dog van in their leathers on a Saturday night. All of them sent her mum into a fit about standards and *looking like they're dressed from the ragbag.*

'Mind if I tag along?' he said.

She shrugged. 'I'm off to buy some clothes. Might not be your thing.'

'Was that Steve I saw you with last Saturday, coming

out of the Odeon?'

'Er, yeah, but don't tell anyone, will you?'

'Why not?'

'He thinks we should keep it quiet, after Lou and all. For a while.'

He made as if to zip his lip, 'What's he got that I haven't?' He bumped shoulders with her. She laughed. 'Look, if there's anything you want from the warehouse...' He glanced over his shoulder, and then lifted the hems of his trousers. There were combs in plastic packets tucked into his socks. He opened his jacket and shampoo bottles bulged in the inner pockets. She felt a rush in her stomach.

'Thanks.' She thought of the radio that Lou had been given; how she'd love one like that.

There was a radio in the kitchen at home, which her mum had tuned to something boring most times. On a Sunday, Sharon and her sisters sat in the kitchen after washing up the tea things and listened to the charts, waiting for the new number one. There were so few times that she could tune in to Radio 1, or Caroline or Luxembourg.

'Not really you, that top,' Steve said when she took her jacket off at the Odeon.

'Oh, it's new.'

'You shouldn't go sleeveless, that's all.'

She slipped her arms into the sleeves of her jacket. She thought it would be attractive, bare skin. Now all she could think of was she'd got it wrong. She leaned into him as the lights went down, and stroked the fabric of his shirt-sleeve between her fingers. He didn't fit a style, wear a badge with his clothes. He was like the dress code signs outside some of the pubs in town: smart casual.

'She phoned again last night, Lou's mum,' he said as they waited for the bus after the film. Sharon was flushed in the face. It was a warm evening, but she daren't remove her jacket and reveal the offending arms. She pulled at the neck of her top to let in some air. 'I don't know what to say to her.'

'What did you say?'

'Told Mum to say I was out.'

'Probably for the best.'

'I do miss her, though.'

'Yes.' Sharon thought how much prettier Lou's arms were, compared to hers.

'She was so pretty, funny. Good to be with, you know?'

Sharon stood in front of the bedroom mirror when she got home, pinching the flesh of her upper arms, checking that she hadn't left any patches on her armpits when she'd shaved. She rummaged through her clothes and picked out all the sleeveless and short-sleeved tops, shoved them in a carrier bag, and pushed it under the bed.

Sharon looked at the clock above the centre checkout as she dashed to the sweet counter: one minute to nine; just on time. She hated that clock. In the last hour on a Saturday afternoon, the minute hand seemed frozen, moving at the rate of the glaciers she'd learned about in geography. Now it meant an hour and a half until tea break.

Steve answered her smile with a nod and a 'Morning, Sharon.' She wondered when it would be all right to say, 'Steve and I are going out together.' She wasn't expecting a full-on snog in the staff canteen, but some acknowledgement – a wink, a glint in the eye.

She pulled a box of chocolate-covered Brazil nuts from below the counter, and tipped some into the Perspex container next to the Quality Street. Paul whizzed by, dipped into the chocolate Brazils and pocketed a handful. She flushed and glanced around. Steve was bundling a box of toothpaste onto toiletries; Mrs Harris was demonstrating the Avery pricing machine to a new girl. Both dashed to the records' counter as The Stranglers clashed across the shop floor. Ralph had broken the rule of playing only the latest *Top-of-the-Pops* not-by-the-original-artists album. Everyone who had the good fortune to be on records gave it a try, playing their favourite record. No-one, so far, had got beyond track one. Meanwhile, Paul bounded up the stairs with a Brazil nut-shaped bulge in his cheek, looking like her brother's hamster.

Steve came over as she was laying out the scoops on the loose sweets. He picked one up and ran it over the top of the chocolate Brazils, as if to smooth them. 'Lou's favourite, these,' he said, and wandered off with a pained look. Sharon took the scoop and dug it into the back of the display.

'You're not your usual self,' Annie Stoker said as they rode the lift to the canteen at lunchtime. Sharon shrugged. 'Missing Louise?' It was the first time anyone had mentioned her in weeks, apart from Steve who talked about her all the time.

She'd had dreams, at first, of worms and bones, even though there was nothing left of Lou but ashes. Then the dreams changed to Lou rising like an angel in a white robe with shining skin and brilliant teeth, slivers of gold light radiating from her fingers.

'I lost a friend,' Annie said, placing her hand on Sharon's back as the lift arrived at their floor. 'You'll feel better in time.' Sharon flinched; Annie Stoker had touched her. Fanny Poker, the other girls called her: the strictest supervisor in the store. Sharon had seen her outside of work once, on the bus to Tadworth, and she was different out of her uniform, friendly. Sharon had thought of telling the others about it, to get them to stop calling her Fanny Poker, but when it came down to it, she laughed along with the rest of them.

They sat at different tables after queuing at the serving hatch: Sharon with Ralph and Paul, Annie with Steve and Mrs Harris. Sharon bit into her roll. The crust collapsed deliciously into the thick slab of cheese and generous spread of butter. 'Not watching your figure?' Steve called across the room. Crumbs tumbled down the front of Sharon's overall.

'Leave that to the boys, eh?' Paul said. He picked up her roll and took a huge bite.

'Oi!' Sharon punched him on the arm.

He broke off two fingers of his Kit Kat and placed them on her plate. 'Fair exchange.'

'I shouldn't.' She glanced at Steve.

'You know you want to.' He waved the Kit Kat in front of her face. She snatched it and put it back on the plate. She nibbled her way through half the cheese roll until Steve left the canteen and then devoured the rest of it, along with the Kit Kat, to a broad grin from Paul.

'You know what you need after that?' he said. 'Sticky bun from Clarks.' She opened her mouth to protest. 'Don't want to hear it. Come on, my treat.'

They both chose Belgian buns, and sat on a bench outside Clarks. 'Has he taken you anywhere apart from the pictures?' Paul said.

'No, but he's taking me to dinner for my birthday.' She unravelled the spiral of pastry and bit off the end of the strip.

'Sweet sixteen and never been kissed.'

'Hardly.' She reddened, remembering Steve's hand inside her bra during *Airport '77*.

'Seriously though, he only takes you to dark places,' Paul said, licking icing from his fingers. 'Except for a disco. You haven't been dancing in ages. Probably find a badly-lit corner of the Berni Inn where no-one can see you. One with cobwebs all around it.' He scrunched the paper bag, and threw it towards a bin. It bounced off the rim and landed on the ground. 'And he's a bit old, isn't he?'

'Twenty-two.'

'Christ, what does your Mum say?' Sharon looked at her feet. 'She doesn't know, does she? Fucking cradle snatcher.'

'Same age difference as with Lou.'

'Serial cradle snatcher.'

There was money missing from the till that afternoon: £5.50. That made eleven fifty-pence pieces in Katrina's bra. Sharon wondered how she distributed them: five in one cup and six in the other, or all eleven warmed by the one boob. Tears welled, and Sharon blushed from her chest up to the roots of her hair as both girls stood in Mrs Harris' office. Katrina looked as she always did, not that anyone could detect a change of colour beneath all that make-up.

'We can't tell for sure if it's a mistake, or if one of you is stealing,' Mrs Harris said. All it would have taken was a metal detector, a miniature version, scanning Katrina's bust. 'So we're taking you both off the tills.' If Sharon told Steve surely he would make it right, get her back on sweets, get Katrina sacked. 'Katrina, you're on toiletries, and you're on gardening, Sharon.' The tills were never out when it was Lou and Sharon on sweets, never. Couldn't Mrs Harris work it out from that? Or maybe she was as dim as Katrina.

Sharon had a card at work the following Saturday, with a big *16* in gold on the front. Everyone had clubbed together to get her three boxes of Matchmakers, one of each flavour, and a Charlie eau de toilette spray. There was no kiss next to Steve's name, but he'd sent her a card in the post with an x on it. Her dad had picked it up from the mantelpiece, and asked, 'Who's this Steve fella?' He'd squeezed the thickly-padded puppy on the front. 'Hope he has a wallet to match.' The puppy had a red collar made of fuzzy fabric.

At morning tea break, Paul sang 'The Wonder of You' and gave her an LP-shaped present. 'Elvis Presley's *40 Greatest Hits*,' he said. 'Thought you needed educating.' She grinned. 'It ain't nicked,' he whispered, pulling a crumpled Harlequin Records bag from his overall pocket. He leaned over, took her hand and kissed it. She giggled.

Steve glanced over from his table, pursed his lips and sniffed loudly, making his nostrils flare. 'Composts are getting low,' he said to Sharon as he left the canteen.

'Not even his floor, why should he care?' said Paul. He helped her load the trolley in the warehouse: boxes of rose food, spades, hoes and rakes wedged upright behind the plastic sacks of multi-purpose compost. 'He's taking the piss, telling you what to do,' Paul said. 'Sorry, gorgeous, but when are you going to wake up to him?'

Sharon shrugged. 'He has to do it, I suppose, so people don't think he's showing favouritism.'

'Bollocks. No-one would suspect you're going out with him, the way he talks to you, and if they did know they'd say the same as me. He's taking the piss.' He hauled open the concertina door of the lift. The metal groaned, and then there was the click of the segs on Steve's shoes as he crossed the concrete floor of the warehouse.

'Aren't you supposed to be breaking up boxes, Paul?'

'Aren't you supposed to stop behaving like an arsehole?' Paul said under his breath.

'What did you say?'

'I said, yes, Sir.' Paul saluted and walked over to the bay where the empty cardboard boxes lay higgledy-piggledy.

Steve snorted. 'Get that stuff onto the shop floor, Sharon.'

'And a happy birthday to you,' Paul said.

'Less of your cheek. When you've finished, Mrs Harris

wants to see you in the office.'

The lift jarred to a halt an inch or two below the level of the floor when it reached Lower Ground. Sharon hauled the trolley backwards up the step, pushed it to her counter, and began unloading and pricing. Blood and bonemeal: the stink from a split sack clung to her hands, her overall, and spilt onto the floor. She walked up to the ground floor to get a dustpan and brush from the broom cupboard. Katrina was leaning towards Steve, holding a small box of nail varnishes, the top two poppers of her overall undone, her cleavage on show. She whispered to him as Sharon walked past. He laughed. Flecks of rooting powder clung to Sharon's overall along with crumbs of compost. She brushed herself down, standing in the broom cupboard. Katrina could behave like a tart as much as she liked around Steve; Sharon was having dinner with him that evening.

Ralph beckoned her over to records. He'd seen Paul in the office with Steve and Mrs Harris; something about stock missing from the warehouse. They'd threatened to call the police. Sharon bit her lip. 'There are only him and his mum at home, you know,' Ralph said. 'She relies on him.'

Sharon waited until Steve was alone, standing with his back to the stairs. 'Paul didn't steal it, that record he gave me,' she said. He shifted from one foot to the other, avoided her gaze. 'He showed me the bag – Harlequin Records.' He gave her that look that said *don't draw attention.* 'So I'll see you later. Half seven?' He nodded, and stepped aside as if to usher her downstairs.

She swept up the mess around the trolley and unloaded the weedkiller. A mirrored badge with the head of Elvis on it had fallen in between the bottles. She closed her palm around it.

All done up in baby-blue eyeshadow, mascara, lipstick and Charlie eau de toilette, she stood in the doorway of Burton's sheltering from the rain. She was in a new floaty dress and jacket, holding a clutch bag, wearing the matching necklace and bracelet of linked hearts that her mum and dad had given her for her birthday. She'd had a bath when she got home, but even with the spray of Charlie a faint smell of compost clung to her. She had placed the Elvis badge in the change compartment of her purse. Sometimes she saw Paul in the High Street of an evening, when she was waiting for Steve.

Steve was late – he'd probably missed the bus – and she'd been early, not wanting to hang around at home once she was ready. Her feet ached. Her stomach grumbled. She'd had a slice of bread and jam to keep her going, when the others had dinner at six, but now she was starving. Hanging around in a shop doorway; her mum would go mental if she saw her, and she knew what her sister Maggie would say: never wait around for a boy.

They'd lose the table, she supposed, if they were late, not that she was used to eating in restaurants. Once, when her dad had a win on the horses, the family had a sit-down meal in the restaurant above the chip shop. She'd had cod, chips and peas on a glass plate shaped like a fish, and there were curved knives with curly lines engraved on them. There was ice-cream for afters in a round silver dish.

She raised the collar of her jacket and ran to the shelter of the bus stop to wait for Steve. The next bus came and went – and the one after that. Her hair was dripping, her tights splashed with grey streaks as passing cars drove through the puddles at the side of the road.

She dashed to the van by the clock tower, and ordered a burger with onions and a portion of chips. She tipped some change from her purse; the Elvis badge fell onto the counter along with the coins. 'That could be a collector's piece now,' the burger-man said, nodding at the badge as he shovelled chips into a paper cone.

'Why's that?' Sharon said.

'Just heard the news on the radio: the King is dead.' Sharon looked puzzled. 'Elvis Presley, found dead at Graceland.'

'Oh my God!' She placed the badge carefully in her purse, along with her change, ate her burger and chips, watched three more buses come and go, and walked home.

Here's Looking at You

'God love you, Janice, you'll make a lovely bride.'
Auntie Joan edged along the pine bench to where
Janice sat, wriggling her arm against Janice's as
she spoke.

The kitchen was filling with women. Janice's mum set
up the glasses with a bottle of Cinzano Bianco and another
of lemonade. She tipped the contents of a jar of lemon
slices and another of cocktail cherries into glass bowls,
which she set on the table either side of a plastic box of
cocktail sticks.

Auntie Joan gulped down half her drink and drew on
her cigarette. A cough rattled round her chest. She had
scarcely regained her breath before rasping, 'So, is there
anything we need to tell you?' She winked in the direction
of Janice's mum who reddened, pursed her lips, shook
out a tea towel, and tucked the top of it into the cutlery
drawer. Janice looked down into her glass. She speared a

cherry with a cocktail stick.

'Sure, I didn't know a thing, the night of my wedding,' Auntie Joan said.

'I knew soon enough when my belly swelled three months later,' Auntie Pam said. Auntie Joan didn't join in the laughter.

Long ago, on summer nights like this, when the Cinzano and the Waterford crystal glasses were lifted out of the sideboard and polished with a dry cloth, Janice had sat in this place, on her favourite, red-topped stool by the coke boiler, and practised becoming invisible, so she could eavesdrop on the women. It was a trick she'd perfected throughout childhood, and it only worked if she clamped her mouth shut. If she spoke, the red-topped stool lost its power, and all eyes turned towards her. *Little ears are flapping,* her mother would whisper to the other women, and then tell Janice to *Go out and play; get some colour in your cheeks. You'll never get a husband with a pasty face.* Now she was one of the women, and less than a day away from having a husband; though the urge to fade into the wallpaper remained.

She spilled a few drops of her drink on the table and stirred it with the cherry-on-a-stick to see if it would go pink. Her mother passed a paper serviette from the pile that was ready to go to the church hall in the morning. It was next to the bride and groom, cushioned in cotton wool in a clear-topped box on the kitchen worktop. Top hat, tails and neat hair for the groom; the bride in a dress that looked so like a bell Janice was sure the little figure would tinkle if she shook it.

She blotted the spill with one half of the serviette, turned it over to see the pattern it had made, and then folded the clean half over the stain. She wanted to see if it would be like one of those butterfly paintings that they used to do at school. Fold a page, paint half a butterfly on one side, then the press the blank side over the painted one. It never worked – one half a shadow of the other, and the painted-in body not enough to hold the split creature together.

'Do you remember Hallowe'en?' Maggie said. 'In the bedroom with the lights out?' Janice nodded at her sister, smiled. 'The idea was to look in a mirror in a darkened room and to see the face of the man you would marry.'

'And did you ever see Phil?' Auntie Joan said. Janice shook her head.

'But there was one year when Dad crept in,' Maggie said. 'The radio was on, so we didn't hear him, didn't know he was there at all till his face appeared beside Jan's in the mirror.' Janice remembered her father's hand on her shoulder, the other at her waist, tickling her that bit too hard, and the face he used to make to scare them as children: one eye screwed up, the other wide open, mouth twisted.

'I remember the screams,' Janice's mother said.

'If we'd known what we were in for in the marriage stakes, wouldn't we all be screaming?' Auntie Pam said.

Her old room was taken up with aunts, and various cousins littered the living room on sofas and cushions. So Janice was to share a double bed with her mother.

The wedding dress was hanging on the wardrobe door where it had lived since she'd collected it after the last alteration. It was the only dress that she owned. On the day she went shopping for it, along with her mother and Maggie, she wore her one skirt, an Indian print. She'd matched the black design on the skirt with thick black socks and clogs. She was pleased with the result when she checked her reflection in the wardrobe mirror. 'You look like Olive Oyl, those skinny legs sticking out of that tatty skirt,' her mother said. She made Janice buy tights in Lilley and Skinner before they got the bus to Kingston, and held up pairs of shoes that would *look lovely* on Janice, none of which did. Janice changed into the tights in the toilets in the car park behind Woolworth's; but still the clogs disappointed. 'I'm afraid she's not wearing the right shoes for trying on dresses,' her mother said to the woman in the wedding dress shop.

'Not to worry,' the woman said. She had hair that didn't move and an orange line where her make-up ended and her skin began. The woman offered a selection of satin shoes with pointed toes and stiletto heels. Janice's mother picked dresses from the rails, responding to grimaces or nods from Maggie as she did so, and passed them through the changing room curtain where Janice waited in her underwear. Help was needed with clasps, zips, and hooks and eyes. The assistant obliged so as not to spoil the effect when Janice emerged through the curtain like a reluctant film star at a premiere. She twirled and turned in a rush of satin and nylon. Each dress made her less like herself, like she was observing someone else in the mirror, a voice in her head saying, *Yeah, nice, if you like that sort of thing.*

'Could we try Laura Ashley?' she said. She had seen some cotton dresses she could live with – floral print, maxi-length. Her mother frowned, and asked the assistant to put a dress aside: the one that had made her reach for the crumpled toilet paper she kept in her bag to dab at her eyes.

'You can't wear one of those,' her mother said as Janice headed for the floral dresses, as though she'd suggested walking down the aisle in the nude. Laura Ashley's wedding section evoked a similar response: 'You couldn't wear a veil with that ... cotton? Why would you be wearing cotton on your wedding day?'

Maggie took Janice aside. 'Look, I've been through this, remember? It's her day as much as yours. When you're married, you can do as you like. It's easier if she has her way.'

Her appetite faded with every shopping trip: florist; hairdresser (for a trial run); to look for a proper pair of shoes; helping her mother to choose her outfit. Two trips for the last of these: regretting her first choice, she needed another, plus a second hat. She then reverted to her first choice, deciding on one outfit for the church and speeches, and another for the disco in the evening. As the wedding arrangements gathered pace, Janice began to shrink. The wedding dress had to be taken in, and taken in again.

Janice *had* slept, though, on the weekends she went home, in between the shopping trips to Kingston, Sutton and Croydon. She'd scarcely had a full night's sleep since she'd met Phil, except when they stayed with one or other set of parents: *my folks* or *your folks*, as Phil called them.

Phil and Janice would lie entwined in her single bed in the Halls of Residence, drifting off after making love, then she'd wake on the border of the mattress, pushed to the edge, and slip to sleep on the rug on the floor with a coat pulled over her, her bones grating on the hard tiles beneath. There was a single bed in his room, too, in the rented house on Clinton Road where the parties of the neighbours in the basement flat rang into the early hours, ending in curses and accusations between the couple that lived there, played out in the middle of the street. Janice would rise to watch the drama through a gap in the curtains: him getting in the car and trying to run her over; her yelling about the *fucking teabags* he'd left on the draining board, then slamming the car door on his leg as he tried to get out to *fucking strangle* her. Phil slept through all of this, night after night, his arms and legs splayed across the bed, and Janice would pull the sleeping bag out of the bottom of the wardrobe and lie on the carpet, littered with tissues and mugs with mould forming across half-inches of tea.

Lie there and listen to the couple's noisy sex, teabags and the urge to kill all forgotten in orgasm after orgasm. Janice wondered what he did to make her scream like that.

She undressed and slipped between the sheets of her parents' bed. There would always be double beds after this – in the hotel the next night; in the holiday flat on the Isle of Wight where they were going for their honeymoon; in Phil's parents' house where they'd be living till they'd saved a deposit for a flat.

She lay on her back and listened to the laughter in the kitchen, glasses clinking in the washing-up bowl, and then the turn of a key and her father's deeper tones added to the half-heard conversation. She opened one eye and looked up at the mirror – the same one in which she had seen her father's reflection at Hallowe'en. It was octagonal with a gold border, and tilted prisms on each edge, so smaller reflections tipped this way and that. She had been fascinated by it as a child, never felt alone when she looked in it.

She dozed, blocking out the bustle below. She could hear water running into a bucket. The floor would be mopped, as late as it was. Janice had taken her mother to a café once. There was a mop leaning against the doorframe of the café's kitchen, and she could see her mother itching to grab the handle and clean up a spill on the floor. She'd contented herself with wiping the crumbs from the table with a serviette and piling the dishes for the waitress.

Light fell onto her closed eyelids. She raised her head and saw her father's reflection in the mirror. 'Jack!' – a whispered shout from her mother. 'Jack! You're in with Kieran tonight.'

The drought broke the next morning. Seven weeks of sun so fierce that the back garden looked like one of those pictures in the geography books, where a lone starving ox stood on the edge of a plain of mud, cracked like crazy paving. Substitute an overfed dog for the ox and with the cracks on a Lilliputian scale, and that was the state of it, only watered by bailed out bath water when someone could be bothered to stir. And along with the rain came Janice's period. She glanced in the mirror at her pale reflection. She reached in her bag for the Feminax, the only thing that touched the pain, though it left her with a not-quite-there feeling. She used to take it when she lived at home, on days where the boredom became too much. Feeling not quite there in this house was a good thing.

The frying had begun in the kitchen; the smell of bacon turned her stomach. A string of bleary-eyed cousins took plates of black pudding, fried eggs and thin circles of liver sausage that curled up at the edge as they fried – like fairy teacups. Janice edged into her place by the boiler, staring at its mottled grey surface, the heavy lid and the metal handle that slotted into it, which could be lifted to throw in the coke. She remembered the heat on her face, the exciting fear of those red hot flames, and the times when, during the power cuts a few years before, her mother had removed that lid and balanced a pan over the hole to fry eggs for their tea.

'Will you have something, Janice?' Her mother's face was glowing. The door was flung open, the windows steamed up, and raindrops were bouncing back from the puddles on the concrete of the back yard. Janice shook her head and clutched her stomach. 'You've never got your visitor?' her mother said. She shoved two slices of white bread under the grill. 'A bit of dry toast, that'll help.'

Maggie walked in with her make-up already on, wearing a wraparound dressing gown over her clothes. 'You'll bake in that,' Janice said.

Maggie shrugged. 'Don't want to get anything on my clothes.'

'It's hours till the wedding.'

'Yeah, but have you thought about the queue for the bathroom? I was in at half seven.'

'Okay, clever clogs, I'll have my bath now.'

'What about your toast?' Her mother was plating up sausages and shouted into the hallway that they were ready. Janice lifted herself from the bench, and looked again at the boiler. She remembered the walk from the bathroom to the kitchen with a Dr White's sanitary towel to burn. STs, her mother called them. Janice would wait in the loo until she felt sure there was no-one to see her carry the bloodied towel, folded – as much as you could fold something the thickness of a nappy – unwrapped, as toilet paper was too expensive to waste.

She ran the taps, and sat on the toilet as the bath filled, with that familiar drag at her abdomen. 'Don't have it too deep,' her mother shouted, 'there are others that need the hot water.' Janice wiped herself and lowered into the few inches of water. There was a knock at the front door. Her mother shouted, 'Maggie, get the door. It'll be the flowers.'

Janice's mother left in the last of the cars, shouting instructions out of the window. The wedding car wasn't due for another twenty minutes, but Janice was not to sit down, and her father was not to mess up anything in the house or spill anything on his tie.

They stood in the shelter of the porch watching the rain pouring from a break in the gutter at the end of the house. 'You and me, kid,' he said, in a voice borrowed from his beloved films: Humphrey Bogart with an Irish lilt. 'Jesus, I look like an undertaker in this get-up.' He faced the hall mirror and grappled with his tie as if loosening a noose. He undid the top button of his shirt. His chest hair curled from the opening. Phil had only three hairs on his chest. He would never be hairy, but she wondered if his belly would swell like her father's, which was straining at his shirt. Janice stood behind her father and straightened his tie until she achieved a reflection that would satisfy her mother. 'Thanks – not too tight, though. She'd have me strangled, that woman.'

'What was it like when you got married, Dad?'

'Now, can I remember that far back?' He winked.

'Come on, tell me.'

'It was…' he paused, 'different.'

Janice walked into the living room and picked up the photo of her mum and dad's wedding from the mantelpiece. Her mother in a powder blue suit, hair piled high on her head, her clear skin unlined, her father impossibly young and handsome, and his tie skewed to one side.

'It wasn't like mine, then – half the town invited.'

He grabbed at her waist and tickled her. She wriggled from his grip. 'You'll be in trouble if you get fingerprints on this dress.' He shrugged, took the photo from her, and replaced it on the mantelpiece.

'Her mother wasn't there. Too many little ones at home to feed – your aunts and uncles.'

'Oh, I didn't know.'

'Just couldn't afford the fares from Ireland.'

'But Nan and Grandad were there, your mum and dad?'

'Oh yes. But there's no love lost between your nan and your mother, as you know; never has been.' He headed towards the sideboard. The door creaked as he opened it. It was the sound that preceded the hospitality her father offered to his friends whenever they called to walk him to the pub. He pulled out two tumblers and a half-bottle of Jameson's, poured a generous measure into each glass, and handed one to Janice. 'Two fingers of red eye at the last chance saloon.'

'Do you remember John Conlon, when he came round

on a Sunday, before you went to the White Horse? How he'd flick his fag ash into the turn-ups of his trousers?'

He laughed silently, his shoulders shaking. 'It was a miracle he never set fire to himself. Ah, he'd have loved to be here today. Absent friends.' He raised his glass.

'Absent friends.' She clinked her glass against his, and they both drained them.

'Funny things, weddings. All dressed up, on your best behaviour, people who can't stand the sight of each other acting like they're the best of friends.'

'And when they've had a few drinks...'

'They dance like lunatics and can't remember a thing the next morning.'

'Or worse...'

'They remember every detail.' He refilled the glasses. 'Yer man Philip was down the White Horse last night. He'll have a sore head today.' Janice's hand shook as she raised the glass to her lips. 'Didn't put his hand in his pocket all evening.'

Failing to buy a round was the worst thing a man could do, in her father's eyes. She finished her drink, and held out her glass for more. Her head was swimming with the effects of the whiskey and the Feminax. She steadied herself with a hand on the back of a chair. 'Mum seems to like him.'

'She likes a wedding. But it's not your mother he's marrying.' He took her glass and placed it next to his on the table. He held her shoulders and scanned her face. 'Look at you. Not five minutes since...' His hands were heavy, resting first, and then squeezing. They seemed so big when she was a child, and still big now, tanned and calloused from years of laying bricks in all weathers. He dropped his hands from her shoulders and grasped hers, turning them palms up, like new velvet being handled by old leather gloves. He let them drop. 'We'll keep a bed for you, if you need it.'

'For me and Phil? We'll be all right at his mum and dad's, until we get our own place.'

'For yourself, if you need it. Though a length of two-by-four would do as a bed, the size of you now.'

Janice bit her lip. 'Can you see Mum taking me in if I come back home after this palaver?'

'Or before this palaver?' He raised his eyebrows. 'We've a car coming soon; where shall we go? Shall we make a run for it?'

'Brighton's nice at this time of year.'

'And we've the proper clothes for the seaside.'

'We might need a brolly.' She gestured towards the rain beating at the window.

He poured another slug of whiskey into each glass, and handed Janice hers. 'Here's looking at you, kid,' he said, raising his glass. Janice tipped her head back and swallowed it down. The car pulled up, and the driver walked up the garden path beneath a large umbrella. Janice lifted her bouquet from the table. 'Ready, Dad?' He took her free hand as she led him towards the threshold.

More Katharine than Audrey

ome Dancing is on Tuesday. Some lose track, but it's mince and potatoes on Monday, *Come Dancing* on Tuesday, sheets changed Wednesday and so on. I'm not supposed to watch it – the lights go off at nine – but I turn the volume low so the staff won't hear. I close my eyes and I dance around the room, then I'm in the black taffeta, and the skirt and my hips are swinging. If the nurses catch me, when they're doing their rounds, their eyes smile above the masks. The flickering of the screen reflects on the walls. My room is a dancehall.

Mrs Davies left the ward today. There are two of us left, so it won't be long until it's my turn. I asked Rankin how far it is to London on the train. It takes half an hour, she said: half an hour from Epsom to Waterloo, and a little longer to Victoria. It seemed to take as long as that to walk the corridors when I first came here. Windows either side, so I could see the grounds and the buildings with the other wards, the laundry and the kitchens. The kitchens are a long way off: sometimes there's porridge, sometimes cornflakes, but always tea and toast, and the toast is cold.

I have my own telly, now that most of the others have gone. There are films in the afternoon: Humphrey Bogart and Katharine Hepburn in *The African Queen*, she as ugly as me, and a film star. It was the other Hepburn, Audrey, that I would have liked to be: petite and pretty, like a fairy gone to live in the world of men. She was a nurse in *The Nun's Story*, tempted by a handsome doctor in a hospital in the Congo; Peter Finch played the doctor. She didn't succumb, but she wasn't for the convent in the end. 'You are a worldly nun,' the Reverend Mother said, or was it the Mother Superior? The times I saw that film and each time the tightness in my chest, a hankie at the ready when she goes into that room at the end of the film, to leave the convent, and she gets her old clothes back, the ones she came in with, and there's no-one there to say goodbye, as if it's a disgrace, wanting to go back into the world.

I could never be like Audrey Hepburn; my hips are too wide.

We had the cowboys back in Mitchelstown – Randolph Scott, Gary Cooper, John Wayne; he was a favourite of Molly's. And I loved Jimmy Stewart. They have them on the telly, too, and it's as if I'm in the middle rows of the picture house with Molly.

I'm like Audrey Hepburn after all, a worldly woman kept apart from the world. She got sick in that film: tuberculosis was it? She was isolated in a beautiful tree-house, given the 'gold cure' and tended to by Peter Finch. And here's me in Long Grove with Rosina Bryars and the nurses. No gold cure for me. No Peter Finch. But it won't be long before they find the right combination of drugs for me, as they did for the others.

Pea soup it said in the books: *six to eight motions a day, and it looks like pea soup.* That's just how it was when I had the fever. I can't eat it to this day: that and rhubarb. Mammy used to boil it up to clean the pans; I worried it would strip the lining of my stomach.

Rankin cut me some roses on Sunday. She brought red and white, but a nurse will always arrange them separately, or there will be blood and bandages before the day's out, so the white went to Rosina and I have the red. They were in bud, so they'd last longer. I've been watching them unfurl. They smell like summer, like the outdoors as I remember it. When the petals drop onto the bedside table, I want them left there to darken, then brown. I want the leaves left to wither on the stem, to watch them shrivel; but the cleaner comes in every day, gloved, overalled, and changes the water, wipes the fallen from the bedside table with a cloth dipped in disinfectant, and it masks the scent of the roses. I close my eyes, and I see the roses in the garden blossom, fade and drop. I walk on a carpet of withered petals, and pinch them between my toes. Then I'm in the field back home with Molly, and we're running fast towards the sun.

Rosina isn't up to much now; she'd as soon eat a rose as smell it.

I was used to the smell of disinfectant when I was nursing, and the way it changes colour in the bucket when you add water. Sid offered me Pernod once, added a dash of water. It clouded in the glass like disinfectant; smelled of the aniseed balls that they tipped into paper bags from the teardrop-shaped bowl of the scales in the sweetshop in Mitchelstown. Disinfectant would do it, if I could get hold of some; I could mix it with the water in my bedside glass and pretend it was Pernod.

There's no wildness in these gardens, just straight lines and fresh mown and leaves piled up in the autumn.

Nothing like the fields back home with the brambles and crab apples. Off we'd go, Molly and me, with bowls to fill, and our arms and our clothes would be torn and purple-bruised with juice. The sweetest would always be the furthest in, and didn't we always want the sweetest, the juiciest, to reach for the best, not to settle?

The first time I offered a brimming bowl to Da, I was so small I had to raise it to reach his hands, hanging like shovel-ends from his arms. He said, no; he wouldn't touch those things, full of spiders and flies. I never offered them again. I gave them up to Mammy for the crumble. His was made separate with crab apples and lots of sugar. He didn't like the black stain on the apples' flesh.

Da thought it was the boys I was after when I went to England. Jesus, with what I've seen of men's parts, what's there to get excited about? Like snails tucked in a hood, and sometimes, sick as they were, it would rear up at the feel of the sponge. God, the first time I saw one at full length I called for Sister. I thought something awful had happened. Shrub came running at my shrieks, and when she saw what had alarmed me, she pursed her lips to stop the giggles. Sister said, 'I think Mr Ericson is well enough to wash himself.' Shrub dragged me into the sluice room and collapsed, tears rolling down her cheeks. Oh, she took me off something rotten: *Sister, come quick it's Mr Ericson's...* I couldn't even find a word to describe it at the time. And we were both in stitches, with her attempt at my accent.

It was last names, even off duty. It was Shrub, Gates, McCallion and so on. You'd say, 'Is Shrub on tonight?' or, 'I've the same shifts as McCallion.' Then the crowd I went round with called me Josie, as there was another Noreen. I forgot I was Noreen at all until I came here; it was in my notes and that's what they go by. I still think of her as Shrub, though she'd a beautiful Christian name – Annette.

But that's how it was, and that's how I remember.

You didn't have to choose what to wear, to be as good as, to have a style. You just wore the uniform, maybe dressed with a frilled cuff if Sister would allow. Rankin wears a cuff and a fob-watch like I had, pinned to the chest. I can see it through the plastic apron. She's my favourite, Rankin; she listens, really listens. Some of them just talk to each other. I suppose we did, too, me and Shrub: tipped the patients forward like they were one of the pillows we were tidying, eased them back, talking over them the whole time. As long as the ward was spick and span, that's what Sister was after.

The fool I was, falling for a woman. I'd study Shrub's lips, the soft hairs on the nape of her neck below her pinned-up hair when she was on the ward, the curl of her hair when it was down, when we went dancing or to the pictures. She hadn't a notion that I dreamed of her, dreams from which I woke with the sheets twisted, dreams of parting her lips with mine, her face cupped in my hands, of slipping a satin nightdress from her shoulders, like the ones they wear in the films, watching it fall to the floor. Sometimes, on the ward, she'd brush against my bosom in passing, and the heat of those dreams would flush my face and neck.

When I first arrived at Euston station from the boat train, no-one smiled or allowed me to catch their eye; no-one said hello. It was just after the war – we weren't involved, in Ireland, so I'd no experience of what they'd been through. Nice enough people, but there was this reserve, and not just because I was Irish. It was as if they'd had something removed, like patients recovering from an operation, trying to get back to normal, but no longer sure what normal felt like. But the nurses, there was a spark in them; they knew how to dance, to drink, to let go. You never knew what you'd encounter on the next shift:

a motorbike accident; a patient with a tumour; a family gathered to hear bad news about their father; and the bed-pans and bottles, everything scrubbed and sterilised. So it was living for the moment.

There weren't always men to dance with, so the women danced together, and if there were any men, the women would flutter round them like moths to an old suit. A man could have a different woman for each dance. I wasn't bothered; if a man asked, I'd dance with him, but I was happiest with Shrub.

So when I went home to Mitchelstown I was full of stories, of the hospital and the friends and the dancing. Mammy clapped her hands and wrung them in turn. She was in envy of me, for getting away and making something of myself; but another part of her was afraid I'd go to the bad. She was wearing her thousand-times-washed dress with the faded paisley swirls of pink and mauve, the lace of her slip peeking out from the hem, and there I was, talking of taffeta and satin and the new coat I'd bought for the winter. As for Da, he was all hard edges, and as broad as he was tall, with no softening at my touch or my words.

I tapped a cigarette from the packet, and tried to light it with the matches from my coat pocket. It had rained on the walk from the bus stop in town, and they were damp, so I put a spill into the embers of the fire. It was as if I'd stripped naked and danced on the table, the blustering and the language from Da, how I'd been ruined by England and nursing. How I was setting a bad example to my sister Molly. I wasn't to smoke either in or out of the house. And when I laid in late, he said, 'There's no holiday here, my girl,' expecting me to go back to my old chores.

I went to a dance at the Mayflower with some of the old crowd, and Jimmy O'Gorman walked me home. He'd been disappointed by a girl he liked; she was dancing with another boy the whole evening. We were great friends, Jimmy and me, and I linked arms with him on the way up the hill. He'd had a drink, and it was as much me holding him up as him walking me home. We parted at the fork in the road below the house.

Da was waiting at the gate, late as it was. 'Are the men in England not enough for ye?' He slapped me round the head. I reeled, but I stood my ground.

'It's only Jimmy. He walked me home.'

'Walking, is it, with everything on show?' We'd had words about how I was dressed before I left the house. I'd wrapped a stole around me to placate him, pinned it with a brooch, but I'd whipped it off at the dancehall. He went for my head again, but I ducked from his open palm. He slapped me round the back of the thighs as he had when I was a child. 'There'll be a different fella every night in London, the hoor you are.'

I flung my head back, the offending bosom thrust forward. I picked up the yard broom and held it in front of me, handle up, to hit him should he come at me again. But Mammy ran out and bundled me inside with Molly. I could hear his old clichés: no daughter of mine and the like. They wouldn't find house room in a decent film script. And I was as bad, battering against the bedroom door with my fists, rattling the handle to get out.

'Mammy locks the door when he has a temper,' Molly said. She looked so small in her nightdress. Her hair hung in waves, released from the plaits they were tied in by day. I came away from the door and sat next to her on the bed. My hands shook as Molly took hold of them. 'Da says I'm not to go to England, but as soon as I've finished school, I'll be away. I want to go to the dances, have all the lovely clothes.' Her hand dropped to my dress, and she rubbed the fabric of the hem between her fingers and thumb. I undressed and got into the bed with her.

'It wasn't so bad when you were here,' she said. 'Could you stay, do you think, until I'm ready to go with you?' I didn't answer. I stroked her hair until she fell asleep, as I used to when we'd shared the bed before I left for England. I lay awake until I heard Mammy making the breakfast for Da, heard him leave for the fields and the turn of the key in the bedroom door, and Mammy going out to draw water from the well.

I slipped from beneath the curve of Molly's arm, gathered my clothes and left. Why would I stay and be beaten and called a whore? Or end up like Mammy, chopping the vegetables, cutting the meat for the stockpot, sweeping the floor, taking out the ashes and sitting on the doorstep waiting for a passing neighbour to bring a bit of gossip.

I sent money home, as was expected, and Mammy wrote letters, begging me to make my peace with Da. I didn't write back, just sent the money. When I came here there was no more money to send.

You'd think, with her being a nurse, she'd know, but they're as prone to such foolishness as anyone, and Annette Shrub fell for a baby. She asked me what should she do, about being in trouble. I said what Mammy would have said: she should get the man to do the right thing.

She asked if I'd be her maid of honour, but I said, 'Can you see me in a froth of a dress with these lumbering hips?' Truth is, I couldn't face the wedding at all. I prayed that her husband-to-be would have a terrible accident and there would be a funeral, not a wedding. Then I hoped that I would break a leg, so I couldn't walk into the church; but the day came and the fella and me were both intact, so the ceremony went ahead. I sat in the front row and stared at her soft neck through the stiffness of her veil. Thinking I might get the chance should her hair become unpinned, and I could caress the stray strands into place, a hair grip in my mouth, press her hair to the back of her head for a second while I reached for the grip. But all went off as planned, not a hair or a word out of place, and Shrub became Mrs Someone-else.

Paper and pen, pen and paper: I ask for them when Rankin brings my dinner – fish pie, as it's Friday – and I start to write home. Someone in the town will know Molly, will recognise the name, even though she might be married now. Someone will know where she lives if she's left Mitchelstown. I keep the letter short, just telling Molly where I am and asking would she like to get in touch, and I ask Rankin to post it. It might take Molly a month or two to write back after a shock like that, a letter after so long.

My hair was good, thick and wavy and almost black, and there was never a problem with my skin. Just those lumbering hips and the bosoms I didn't know what to do with. Cover them up, Mammy would say, though the devil in me said show off your assets. The men had a fair love of them. When I wore the black taffeta with the red roses and a glimpse of cleavage – a glimpse was all they needed – some of them couldn't keep their eyes away as they asked for a dance. I wanted to tilt their chins with the heel of my hand, so their eyes would be level with mine. How they'd have loved to get their hands on my chest. It wasn't their hands I wanted.

Annette gave me a photo: bride and groom, beauty and the beast. I cried over it every night until I could bear it no more. I burned it in the sink, watched the faces blacken and curl, and then rinsed the ashes down the plughole.

Shrub gave up on the dancing, so I went with McCallion instead. I wore the black taffeta with roses again that night, black stockings, heels, my hair up with a mother of pearl clip, and red lipstick to match the roses on the dress.

This man came over, and it was me he was interested in, not McCallion, though she was the slimmer and prettier of the two of us. I danced with him, but it was Shrub I thought of: how I would tuck my hand close around her fingers as I swung her, pull her close, push her back, the lightest of touches as she twirled beneath my arm, her finger looped in my finger and thumb, and her skirt flying, her hair streaming behind her, and the set of her mouth as she concentrated on the steps, and the click of her heels on the dance floor, the lightest of clicks – click-click – and the flush of her cheeks as we fell back to the table for our drinks.

He was kind, this man Sid – older than me, well spoken, a proper English gentleman – and we fell into a courtship of sorts.

When I get out of here I'll take a flat in Tooting Bec, be close to things. I'll wander round the market with my basket in the morning, stop for a cup of tea and a slice of toast and jam at Luigi's café, maybe look up Shrub, if I can remember her last name (what was the name of that fella she married?). Or just sit in the café and wait for Godot. He took me, that Sid who courted me, took me to the theatre to see it. Hadn't a clue what it was about – two old tramps talking and waiting for a man that never turned up. I didn't get it. Much preferred a bit of a musical when I went to see a show, or to go for a meal and a swing round the dance floor.

I could do that, too: take a look at a dancehall in Kentish Town, go and watch the young ones, maybe show them a few moves myself! I'll need a new wardrobe. It won't be like Audrey Hepburn in *The Nun's Story*, they won't give me back the same clothes that I came in with. They'll have been incinerated. And decades out of fashion in any case. Any old rags, they give you here; the Lord only knows where they find them. But I keep up with the trends in the magazines that Rankin gives me after she's read them. I suppose she's not allowed to take them out of here anyhow, but it's good of her nonetheless.

The food came and it was grand: steak, fried, fancy potatoes done with cream and thin slices of onion, a little salad of lettuce, tomatoes and cucumber in a glass dish of its own at the side of the main plate, and cloth serviettes embossed with an ivy leaf motif. I dove in with my fork turned the wrong way. Sid smiled, turned it round in my hand and showed me how to push the peas onto the fork, to soak the gravy with a little potato on the prongs.

He ate like a lady, little bites. And he stared at me, a shine in his pupils, but it was the food that got me going, not him. It was all I could do to stop lifting the plate and licking it clean. After Shrub married, I got so thin that my curves all but straightened, but my appetite returned that night. And a hand on my knee beneath the table, which did nothing for me, but I let him.

He took me dancing in Kentish Town, fingers pressing into my back in the slow dances, his cheek to mine, and his cigarette breath on my neck. We twirled round the hall, and my frock swirled and flicked, and he smiled.

That was the night he gave me Pernod. I wasn't much of a drinker, in spite of what Da thought of me, and I warmed to Sid with the drink inside me. I placed a hand at his back as we walked from the taxi, leaned my head on his shoulder. He turned to kiss me. His moustache scratched at my top lip. It was cold, raining; we sneaked past his landlady's door. There were drips coming through the ceiling in the attic room, pots and pans laid out to catch them. He drew me onto the bed beside him, slipped the dress from my shoulders and kissed my neck. His face was red; he was breathless. I shouldn't have led him on so.

That was the night that did for me: someone in the kitchen of that restaurant. Someone that was a typhoid carrier like I am now, not washing their hands, passing it on to all that ate there.

The daylight is fading. I have to wait for the lights to go on. I'm down to the last page of the *Daily Mail* with those pictures: men on the moon, looking like they're underwater in diving suits, and more men at Houston staring at screens, pencils dangling from their fingers like cigarettes.

If I had a suit like that I could go into town and shop for myself at Woolworth's instead of asking Rankin to get bits and bobs for me. I could get a cup of tea and a jam tart at a café. Last night I dreamt of cafés and pubs and shops and crowds, of sliding into a seat on the top deck of a bus, arms and thighs butted up against the woman in the window seat, carrier bags arranged around my feet. A bit of food from the International Stores, a pair of tights, a new blouse, a lipstick, tickets in my handbag for the stalls at the Odeon from the night before, a dab of perfume behind my ears.

I wouldn't be able to drink the tea, I suppose, in a spaceman's suit.

I asked for some knitting needles and wool, and I am clicking my way through a scarf, russet and green, to match the coat I have picked out from the *News of the World* magazine. I don't want to order it; I'll wait till I can try it on. I could try knitting gloves, but they're tricky.

Rankin brought me a box of Christmas cards. I've written one for Rosina, one for Rankin, some for the other nurses and for Mavis the cleaner. There's been no reply to the note I sent Molly in the summer. I'll try again, with a card. I choose a holy one with the blessed Virgin and the infant Jesus, haloes lighting their faces. I give it to Rankin to post.

Love

When I came home that evening, there was a man sitting on my garden wall, drinking tea from a mug and eating a thick-cut sandwich. His hair was long and matted, and those parts of his flesh that I could see were muddy brown, either through exposure to the elements or a lack of soap and water. He rose a few inches as I walked up the steps to the door, each of us glancing sideways, neither of us looking at each other, then he sat back down to finish his meal. Later, there was the drained mug, the tooth-marked remains of a ham sandwich and a brown stain on the path, which I had no interest in identifying.

The post that morning had brought a card from Spain. I should have felt pleased for them, the girls at Eagle Star, and glad that they'd remembered me. Instead I buried the card beneath leftover Weetabix and coffee dregs in the kitchen bin; a postcard to an alien, like viewing a world where I no longer belonged.

It had seemed a good idea, the year before, to move from Eagle Star, where I'd worked so long I'd almost taken root, like one of the office plants. Thought I'd take a risk and try a new career in marketing. And I'd liked it at the new place; but then they had to make cuts, and it was last in, first out. So I was not only an alien, but a redundant one, who hadn't worked long enough at Can-Do for a pay-off.

There was a folk festival in town, and I decided to go along, as a distraction from sinking into self-pity. The town was full of aliens, so I felt right at home. The day was billed as Ruby Tuesday, and everyone was supposed to wear something red. I found an old red T-shirt and blended in with the other aliens with red streaks in their hair and beards, and painted eyebrows. After I'd had my fill of Morris dancing, I came home to this tramp – if we're allowed to call them that these days. Gentleman of the road, homeless person, whatever he was, I hadn't seen him around before. You notice them, people from other alien races, when you're an alien yourself, but they're invisible to most people – until they sit on your garden wall.

It's a balancing act between safety and charity. Who knows, Mr Tramp might be a violent sort. But the words of that bible passage filtered through, the one about faith, hope, *and the greatest of these is love:* not charity, love. Someone had shown this man love and directed him to my garden wall café for his snack. I suspected my neighbour, a practising Catholic. For me, being a Catholic was like my efforts to learn the violin. I gave up both in my teens. It wasn't as though you worked hard and arrived at perfection. You had to keep practising – not worth the sacrifice for the returns.

When I went through my charitable phase, my love phase, I volunteered at the Simon Community, a home for the homeless. Some of the men travelled around the country, signing on at different towns, and came to Kent for the summer. It was like a holiday for them. There isn't much begging now, what with *The Big Issue,* but in those days they'd stretch out their hands for the price of a cup of a tea. Never went on tea, of course, straight to the off-licence for a can of Special Brew.

I wondered where Mr Tramp thought of as home. I couldn't ask him; my days of 'love' were over. I didn't know where I belonged anymore than he did. Not in the house where I was raised: I'd said goodbye to that years ago. Mum was still there, of course, but it had been months since we'd spoken, not since Dad's funeral when I said I wouldn't go. There were tears from her, and just three words, 'How could you?' That's what I thought, too, how could you put up with that for all those years? Self-love, or a lack of it, that's what it came down to.

I remembered the parties, when he brought people back from the pub. He would turn up the Dansette, and get Mum to make sandwiches for his cronies. I lay in bed praying for the house to stop whooping and the floorboards to stop shaking. There was always the Dubliners, 'Seven Drunken Nights' and 'The Black Velvet Band', then the songs about leaving Ireland or going back to that "Old Irish home, far across the foam". If Ireland was that great, why didn't they go back and live there?

When you're English, but your family's Irish, you never know where you belong, where home is. England was where we lived, but Ireland was home, even though we kids had only ever been there on holiday. Maybe that's why I've always felt like an alien.

You know how once you've noticed someone, you see them all the time? Well, Mr Tramp turned up again, sunbathing on the grass verge near Matalan, a stuffed carrier bag beneath his head, a can of White Lightning clutched in his fist. I wonder if my dad would have ended up like that if it weren't for Mum. The word 'alcoholic' was never used in our house. Dad was a man who liked a drink, good company down the pub, same as the uncles who came over from Ireland to live with us for a while until they got settled. They'd come over happy and full of life, greeting people they met on the street, like they would at home. No-one replied. Mum told them *don't go round saying hello to everyone; they don't do it over here.* After a while they didn't smile so much, and the drinking started.

Only once did Mum come close to admitting that Dad had a problem. 'It's a disease, you know,' she said. She'd got friendly with one of the nuns, Sister Anne, at the Convent of the Sacred Heart where I went to school. Sister Anne told Mum about Al Anon, a support group for the families of alcoholics. They met every Friday night in the school hall. Mum wouldn't go in case the neighbours found out and, in any case, Dad did go on the wagon once in a while, so he wasn't really an alcoholic, or so she said. Those times were worse than the drinking – him finding fault with everything and hanging round the house not knowing what to do with himself. And Mum seemed to lose the hold she had on keeping the family going. Servicing an alcoholic was her job; she was redundant when he stopped drinking.

I never had the urge to travel when I was a teenager, the way that young people do; the way that homeless people do. The summer after A-Levels, I got as far as St Ives in Cornwall, working in a shop that sold seashells and tacky gifts. Thought I'd visit the English holiday world. I'd only ever been to Ireland in the summer holidays, plus day trips to the coast, the annual outing to Littlehampton with Dad's Working Men's Club. Then, on my nineteenth birthday, I went to work at Eagle Star, where I did the nine-to-five for twenty years. Two weeks in Spain once a year with the girls from the office, and onto the property ladder, using each pay rise to overpay the mortgage. Then sense went out the window when I changed jobs at forty.

Maybe I'd become a traveller now. I'd heard about the adult gappers, people who sell everything and go round the world. There was nothing to keep me here. I did some research on the internet, bought some guidebooks. I fancied New Zealand. It looked good in *The Lord of the Rings* films. I even had the house valued.

Mr Tramp was gone by the end of the summer, holiday over, back to the grindstone of doing whatever tramps do. My brief flirtation with wanderlust was over, too. I took a bus into town to pick up the Adult Education brochure. It's what I call my seasonal adjustment, looking for something to do as the nights draw in. There was a *Big Issue* seller by the bus station. He was wearing a thin jacket, holes in his shoes. It was drizzling and cold. He had his dog with him, tied to the railings, a blanket thrown over it, a plastic tub of water by its head. A woman in a coat with a fur collar was shouting at him: 'Are you going to keep that dog out all day? And does it have somewhere to sleep at night? I hope you're feeding it properly.' It was the week that a whale had got stranded on the banks of the Thames and pages of newsprint were devoted to the tragedy. Meanwhile a new drug for Alzheimer's had been declared too costly to be dispensed to those that needed it. It struck me that there wasn't much love in the world.

I barged in front of the screeching woman. 'How much for all your copies?' He quoted a sum. I searched my pockets, gathered up all my notes and change and stuffed them into the young man's hand. 'Get yourself home,' I said.

Biddy

When Jack, Noreen and I came home from school that day, there was a man we didn't know drinking tea with Mammy and Daddy. 'Jack, your father's come to visit,' Mammy said, and then to me and Noreen, 'This is your Uncle Seamus, say hello.' The man sat at the table, broad-shouldered, legs wide, and he opened his arms for Jack to go to him, but Jack stood firm, as if he were stuck to the flagstones, arms pinned to his side. 'Now say hello,' Mammy said again, and me and Noreen spoke, but Jack wouldn't say a thing.

Mammy sent us out to do our chores, but Jack was to stay there, and when we came back he was standing by the fire, poking it with a stick, whilst Uncle Seamus talked and talked. I hung about by the doorway, quiet, so I wouldn't be noticed, to see what I could learn.

Uncle Seamus had a grand job as a market gardener and Aunt Maggie kept house, looking after Caitlin, the child they'd had in England. They lived in a town called Epsom where there were lots of horses, on account of the racecourse, and it had a cinema and dancehalls and a railway station. Uncle Seamus showed Jack picture postcards of the town, so he could get to know it. This was where Jacky would live once his schooling was finished.

Jack wouldn't shake Uncle Seamus' hand when he left; he wouldn't look at him at all. 'Shake hands with your daddy,' my daddy said.

'He's not my daddy,' Jack said.

'He is so. Now I won't have bad manners in this house. Say goodbye to your daddy.'

'You're not my daddy, you're not,' he shouted at Uncle Seamus, and ran across the room and kicked him.

My daddy picked him up, with his legs flailing. Uncle Seamus stood up and smoothed his hair down, like it had been no more than a fly that had landed on him, and he picked the watch out of the pocket on his waistcoat that hung on a chain clipped to another pocket. 'You're not my daddy, you're not,' Jack yelled while my daddy carried him outside, and we heard the sound of the belt whizzing through the air.

'You're to go in now, Jack, and shake hands with your daddy.' But the belt kept whizzing and the hard thwack as it hit Jack's behind, and Jack never spoke a word or uttered a cry, and in the end Uncle Seamus had to leave to get the boat, and still Jack wouldn't shake his hand or speak to him.

As we settled down to sleep that night I could hear Jack snivelling, see his shoulders shaking in the glow of the firelight that crept through the gap in the door from the kitchen. 'Is that man your daddy, Jack?' I asked.

'Sure, I don't know that fella at all.'

He never came again, Uncle Seamus, just that once, but he kept sending the money for Jack's keep and picture postcards. Aunt Maggie never came at all.

I suppose it was the visit of Jack's youngest daughter, Janice, that brought me back to the day I discovered that Jack wasn't my brother. It was strange weather for February when she came. Warm enough to go without a jacket when we came into town to meet her. All I knew of her was the letter saying she was visiting Mitchelstown, and she'd liked to meet me. I wasn't sure I wanted to. My Joe and I don't leave the farm much these days. The town's too busy for us, and there's the new road and roundabouts; Joe gets all flustered, he doesn't drive much these days. We said we'd meet her at the Clongibbon Hotel, Sunday roast, though she had something without the meat.

She was like my Aunt Alice, her grand aunt, handsome women both. You could see it in her eyes, her hair, the resemblance passed from one generation to another. Alice, behind the counter of her sweetshop in Upper Cork Street, hair pinned back, high-necked blouse, measuring sherbet pips into the bowl of the scale that was shaped like a pear drop. And this girl, Janice, even with her hair cut short like a boy's, had the same wave in her hair and Jack's smile, his height, his pale blue eyes. She showed me photos of her own girls; no mistaking they were Irish, in spite of their English daddy.

'Do you have any photos of my dad?' she asked. I'd none of him as a boy, but there was one of him in his uniform.

He'd gone to Uncle Seamus and Aunt Maggie as soon as he'd finished school. Two years later, he came back home, to Mitchelstown, in an RAF uniform. Oh, he looked fine! He'd been sent on National Service, though my daddy said he couldn't see what service England had done for any of us. It was just after the war, but it wasn't our war;

our war was with the English, as my father saw it. How often had he told us the story of Mitchelstown Castle, built in the image of Windsor, just one window less? That night in 1922, a patriot set fire to the castle, the home of the Kingstons, the English landlords, and Daddy had stood at the foot of the town watching the flames on the hill above. He could hardly look at Jacky in that uniform.

Jacky hated National Service. He talked about having to run at sacks made to look like hanging men, to thrust his bayonet in their straw guts, shouting all the while. It made him sick to the stomach that he might have to do that to human flesh.

Janice had the look of an Irish girl, but with an accent that didn't fit, well-spoken you'd call it, and fidgety, fingers moving all the time, legs shifting, chewing at her lip. She asked for decaffeinated coffee and the waiter said, 'I'll go and see if we have any'. Once the fella was out of earshot, Joe said, 'Sure, you'll have decaffeinated, whether they've got it or not, and he'll ask if you can you taste the difference.' She laughed then for the first time. 'So it's your first time in Mitchelstown?' he said.

'Yes. I've been to Ireland before, though, when I was little: every second summer in Ennistymon, where Mum grew up.'

'So what's made you come now?' I asked.

'I've been thinking about it since Dad died. I was helping Mum to clear his things, but we couldn't find anything from his childhood – no birth certificate, no photos. He'd no mementoes of Ireland at all.'

'That's how it was back then. You left with the one suitcase. And we'd not much to start with.'

There were posters up asking for girls to go and work in England. My sister Noreen had gone ahead to London to train as a nurse. There was a fierce row when she came back for her holidays; she wanted to smoke in the house and be out all hours at the dances. She was used to pleasing herself. But Daddy wouldn't have it. She went back to London early, and we had no letters from her after that. The ones Mammy sent her were returned marked *not at this address.* So when I raised the idea of going to England, there were arguments, with Daddy saying I'd take on bad ways like my sister. Mammy wrote to Aunt Maggie to arrange a job near where she lived, so she could keep an eye on me, and I didn't mind 'cause I could be near Jacky.

It's all about not doing what your mother did at that age. Seventeen, I was, when I left for Dun Laoghaire with a suitcase packed with two of everything. Sailing away to escape the life my mother had, sitting on the front step after sweeping it in the hope of a bit of gossip from a passing neighbour. England meant freedom, a chance to earn some money of my own, but when I got there, I didn't like the taste of the tea.

I was a mother's help in a big house in Banstead, a room thrown in with the job. Nobody understood what I was saying! When I said to the young boys I was looking after that they were *very bold,* the missus chastised me, told me to speak English, and so I learnt: *naughty,* not bold. And then she sent me to the market for carrots and swedes. Well, in Ireland we called swedes 'turnips'; I didn't know what she was after. I was too shy to ask, hoping that I'd pick out swedes, whatever they were, for myself. But the boy on the stall became so vexed with me that he took my basket and filled it with potatoes. 'Here you are, Biddy, you know what they are.' I almost forgot my own name, the times I was called Biddy. Another time, the missus told me to make a rice pudding. I'd never seen rice in my life! But I found a cookbook in the kitchen, and somehow I managed.

Oh, that woman was so particular! She docked my wages when I scorched the wee one's vest with the iron, then put it on him. Sure, no-one would have seen it beneath his jumper, but she decided it wasn't for wearing. Then she knocked the broom out of my hand when she saw me dusting the floor with the vest wrapped round the bristles, threw it clean away when it was fine as a duster.

I sent half my wages home to Mammy, as was expected, and I wrote letters saying how grand it was in England, but all the time my heart was breaking.

'I've not had much luck with the parish priest,' Janice said, 'he wouldn't let me see the register.'

'It's the Americans,' I said. 'They come over looking for their Irish relatives. They tear pages out of the parish records.'

'God, that's awful.' She lifted her cup, her hand shaking, and spilt some coffee in the saucer. Then she started fussing with a tissue from her handbag, mopping up the spill.

'What I really want to know,' she said, 'is why he was left behind. Why he was brought up with you and not in England with my nan and granddad.'

'That wasn't unusual,' Joe said. 'They would have gone over to find work and somewhere to live. And you can be sure that wherever they found, it wouldn't be suitable for a baby.'

'But why leave him all that time? Why not send for him when they found somewhere suitable?'

'The arrangement was that Uncle Seamus sent money for your father's schooling and that he would go to them in England when he was sixteen,' I said. 'But he didn't know them, not really. He went to live with strangers.'

'But how could you do that? Leave your child?' she said.

What could a girl with a cushioned life like hers know of what it was like in those days?

I remember walking across the heath at night, after getting off the bus from the picture house in Epsom, on a night as black as the devil's soul; those boys calling after me and taking the rise out of my accent when I shouted back at them. And there was no comfort when I got in. Treated like the servant I was. And the boys' father couldn't keep his eyes to himself. He was forever sidling up; standing in the kitchen doorway watching me as I made the boys' tea; peering down the stairs late at night when I came back from an evening off; brushing past me in the hallway. It didn't go unnoticed by the missus. She found even more faults with my work, more chances to shout at me, to stop my money: an old cup whose handle broke off in the soapy water of the kitchen sink; burning the boys' toast. I was jumpy, ready to drop a dish, knock the bucket over when he crept into the kitchen as I knelt down scrubbing the floor.

Then it got so it wasn't just his eyes he couldn't keep to himself. It was none of my wanting, but there was no such word as 'no' as far as he was concerned. At first it was a touch of the arm, a pat of the behind – brazen, when the missus was in the room, but had her back turned. My cheeks were permanently flaming when he was around, and the missus glared at me as if it were my fault when his eyes rested on my chest. As it was, I had never learned about the birds and the bees. Mammy hadn't explained a thing. The first time I got my monthly visitor I was scared to death! I'd worked out, somehow, that there were parts of me that were private, that no-one was to touch.

It was just the once that he caught me, when I was back late from the picture house. He came downstairs in his pyjamas. He started with the hand on my arm, as usual, and he pushed me into the kitchen and closed the door behind him. He had me off my feet, my back on the table. He ripped my stockings, pulled aside my knickers, and he pushed himself between my thighs. All I could do was concentrate on the tin of Vim next to the sink – Vim, Vim, Vim, the word going through my head again and again, and the thought of scrubbing the sink in small circles, and the smell of the loaf on the table behind me, turned cut side down on the bread board with a knife next to it that I could have used if I'd have had the nerve. 'You like that, don't you, little Biddy?' he said, and I decided to be Biddy. It was Biddy, not me, who was on the kitchen table with this man with the red and white striped pyjama bottoms round his ankles, which I'd have to wash next Monday morning, soaking away the marks of my blood on the hem of his pyjama top with cold salt water.

'He was bright enough,' I said. 'He could have stayed on to do the Leaving Cert. But the agreement was that he'd go to England when he was sixteen.'

'And he ended up labouring,' Janice said. 'He was frustrated by that, could have done something with his brains.'

'Ah, there are many Irish brains carrying hods on the building sites of England,' Joe said.

'And he wasn't proud or interested at all when I got a place at university; he said I should be out earning money.'

'Well, you can understand,' Joe said. 'You were doing what he wasn't able to.' He called for the bill, waved away Janice when she opened her purse to pay. 'You're on your holiday. Put your money away.'

We drove her to the schoolyard, the church, out of town and up to the old house at Stag Park. Different now – an extension with a proper kitchen and bedrooms, the garden fitted out with a swing and a slide. Mick Cusack, the man who owns the house now, was digging in the garden, his wee son standing in his shadow, the same height as Jacky was the day that Uncle Seamus came. 'My daddy used to live here,' Janice said to the boy. Her eyes were filled with tears; I pretended not to notice. She swallowed hard, and asked if I'd take a photo of her by the house.

'I was reared here, too,' I said to Mick. 'There were just two rooms then. No running water. We'd to fetch the water in barrels with a donkey and cart.' I told some stories of those days, of how my father taught his grandfather to dance, so he could go courting. Then we shook Mick's hand and waved goodbye to the boy.

She wanted to see the graveyard, where my mammy and daddy are buried. And she asked if we could persuade the priest to show her the register: with us being known to him he might oblige.

My monthly visitor didn't arrive. I used to suffer dreadfully, doubled over, blinding headaches, and it didn't always come when it should, so I thought little of it; then nothing again the next month. I was too mortified to go to Aunt Maggie. Holier than the Pope, attending Mass every Sunday and all the Holy Days of Obligation, taking her turn with doing the flowers and the cleaning at St Clement's – she'd send me back to Ireland if she knew. I'd heard about girls back home being sent away and never seen again if they got into trouble. Mammy had said I'd go to the bad in England; I didn't want to prove her right. I suppose I pretended that nothing had happened, that if I ignored it, everything would work out fine.

I'm sure the missus knew what had passed between me and her husband. Nothing said, but looks and finding fault. Thank God he didn't come near me again. He kept out of my way; she kept him out of my way. He acted like I didn't exist.

I went round to Aunt Maggie's to tell Jacky I was fed up of the job, of being bossed around. I was going to try my luck in London. I'd heard there was work to be had in a biscuit factory in Peckham.

Aunt Maggie had an apron tied round her, and pastry rolled out on the table, dropping crinkled rounds into a baking tin. Jacky's little sister, Caitlin, was dipping her finger in the jam, and her toys were all over the kitchen and the living room. Jacky cast a look at the child and pursed his lips. 'She's very bold,' he whispered to me. But Aunt Maggie thought she was the sun, the moon and the stars; she wouldn't have her told off.

He was working all over the place by that time, going off in a van with a load of Irishmen he'd met at the Tara Club, to find whatever labouring they could: Bedford, Bracknell, wherever they could travel in a day, setting off before it was light, working until the daylight failed, back after dark, then straight to the pub. I wanted the brother I thought he was when we slept in the same room of the house at Stag Park, listening to Mammy and Daddy in the other room talking until the fire embers dimmed. But all he was interested in was work and the drink and a flutter on the horses.

I liked the factory; there were other girls to talk to, and the radio played all day to make the time pass quicker. I stayed at Aunt Maggie's for a while, travelling up and back to work by train. Let's just say I wasn't made to feel welcome, and Caitlin had me driven half mad with her spoilt ways. So I walked the streets looking for a boarding house closer to the factory. Those were the days of the signs in the windows: *No blacks, no Irish, no dogs.* And even those that didn't have signs – as soon as I opened my mouth and they heard my accent they'd say they they were no vacancies after all: no room at the inn. But I made friends with an English girl called Ivy, and she told me of a woman that would take me in. 'It's clean enough, and cheap,' she said. 'And the landlady, Mrs Broughton, she helps girls out, if you know what I mean.' I was so green my only thought was that she took in girls like me who had nowhere to stay.

Some secrets should stay buried. Shaking the earth from the roots of the past can turn up parasites, infecting those that choose to do the digging. There, in the pages of the parish register, Jack's baptism, 14th of July 1928, parents: Margaret Condon, Seamus Flaherty. Janice searched backwards and forwards – no record of their marriage.

'They must have left for England soon after Dad was born,' she said. 'I suppose with Nan's sister, your mum, already married…'

'They'd have passed Jack as their own.'

'But why did they go, why not stay and get married?'

'That's the way it was,' I said. 'If a child was born out of wedlock, the woman had to leave.'

'All that *stand, sit, kneel* in St Clement's every Sunday. And all the time Nan was… and Dad was…'

I was at the factory when it started. There was blood and the most terrible pain, like a fist had closed on my insides then spread its fingers wide. I thought of what Jack had said about sticking his bayonet in the man made out of a sack, twisting it.

Ivy took charge, said to the foreman that I was sick and couldn't get home by myself. Then she took me to the hospital. She waited by the curtained-off bed, and then a nurse came in. 'Oh dear,' she said, 'we don't look very comfortable, do we?' and she arranged my pillows, though it seemed to me like there was nothing that would help, short of the intercession of the Blessed Virgin. I was sweating; the cramps were coming faster, more painful each time. She said something about breathing, and she let me grip her hand as a wave of pain seared through me, and she rubbed my back all the while. No-one had touched me in a gentle way in a long time, not since I'd said goodbye to Mammy and Daddy when I left for England.

When the pain eased a little, the nurse picked up the chart clipped to the end of the bed and asked my name, date of birth and so on. Her back stiffened, and her lips clamped shut into a tight line when I told her my address.

They wheeled me to a room; Ivy was told to wait outside. The doctor came, and the nurse showed him the chart and whispered something to him. 'It seems that whatever you've had done is taking its course, Miss, er...' He spat out the word 'Miss'. I had no idea of what he meant or why he handled me so roughly. He muttered a few words to the nurse, and left.

She laid a sheet beneath me, placed another over me, and spoke under her breath about clearing up other people's mess. Then she left me to get on with the business. I called after her to ask Ivy to come in, but she closed the door behind her without a backwards glance.

'Was it known, that he was illegitimate?' Janice said. I remembered the words they used at school: *a boy child* or *a girl child* for those who had no daddy, for those who lived with their aunts, for those whose grandmother raised them as their own. I remembered the whispering about Jack at home, the taunting at school.

'No, it wasn't known,' I said.

A Coffee and a Smoke

Maura enjoyed a certain freedom since Jack had died. With the advent of Freeview, the telly had been permanently tuned to *Sky Sports News*. Now she could watch last night's *Emmerdale*, or catch an old film on TCM. She could eat when she wanted (diabetes permitting), and have a tray in front of the telly, even at breakfast. There was no need to set the table for one.

She washed up one bowl, one side plate, one cup and saucer, and pulled back the net curtain. The rain blurred her view of the houses across the street. It was days like these that reminded her of home: *a soft day*, her father used to call it.

Two brown envelopes and a postcard dropped through the letterbox. *Greetings from Tralee;* that would be from Jim-the-Milkman. He'd long since left United Dairies, and retired back home, to Ireland, but Jim-the-Milkman he remained whenever she thought of him. She stopped herself from turning the card over. She'd save it for later, enjoy it over a coffee and a smoke.

The terrier that danced round her feet retreated when she opened the door. 'Scared of getting your feet wet, are you? Big baby.' She picked him up and held him close to her face until he squirmed. 'Come on now, Lester, it's only a bit of rain.' She clipped a lead to the metal loop on his collar and put on her raincoat. They walked down the alley at the back of the houses trying to avoid Joan. She'd be bound to join them, and once Maura and Joan got talking, that would be half the day gone. Maura wanted to get to the shops and there was the business of Jack's things to sort out later on. Only a pint of milk and a small loaf needed: strange sensation, the weight of two items in her shopping bag. It used to be seven at the table every night, and the milk was delivered daily: four pints, then three, then two, then down to one every other day. She'd stopped having the milk delivered after Jim-the-Milkman retired, had only kept it going for him, for the chance to catch up on the gossip and to reminisce about home over a coffee and a smoke. Home... it would always be home, even though she'd lived in England for fifty years.

Joan's back door opened. There was no fooling her; she knew what time Lester had his walk. 'Hold on,' she shouted. She flew out, buttoning her jacket, and caught up with Maura and the dog in the alley. 'Lester Piggott, how are ya?' The dog leaped at Joan, licking her hands. Maura pulled his lead tighter, drawing him close to her side, and Joan linked arms with her. 'It was a grand night, wasn't it?' Joan said, lowering her head against the rain. They nodded in unison. 'Sean Burke was on good form,' Joan said.

'Ah, yes! When he sang "The Cliffs of Doneen"...'

'Sure, I was there myself.' Joan began to sing, 'You may travel far, far from your own native home...' and Maura joined in, 'Far away 'cross the ocean, far away 'cross the foam.' By the time they reached the park, they were in full voice for the chorus. A woman with a buggy gave them a disapproving look. 'Morning,' Joan said. The woman adjusted the hood of the buggy, as if protecting the child from the two women, and passed in silence. Joan and Maura collapsed into laughter as soon as she was out of earshot. 'She'll be telling yer man that she met two mad old Biddies in the park,' Joan said. Maura retrieved the crumpled tissue, tucked into the sleeve of her cardigan, and wiped a tear from the corner of her eye. 'Do you remember when you first came over?' Joan asked.

'I do.'

'How you used to say hello to everyone you met, same as at home?'

'Yes, and they'd look at me like I should be locked up.'

'And one day you said "Howya?" to this young girl…'

'And you said "Howya?" back.' Warmth spread over Maura's shoulders, the familiar story like a comfort blanket.

They were halfway round the park. Maura's arthritic hand was beginning to seize up, and Lester was tugging on the lead. She changed it to the other hand and flexed her fingers.

'Give it here,' said Joan, taking the lead from her, 'and put your gloves on. You know you've to keep your extremities warm, with the diabetes and all.'

'Aren't you the bossy one?'

'Ah, keep quiet now, and let yourself be looked after.'

Maura scowled, but put her gloves on.

'So, what excitement have you planned today?' Joan asked.

'Ah, lunch at the Ritz, berate the servants for not polishing the silver properly … the usual.' Maura pulled her shoulders back and head up as she spoke.

'Me too,' said Joan.

Maura hoped that Joan wouldn't invite herself for lunch. She wanted to catch up on her soaps, have a snooze with the dog draped on the back of her armchair. 'Actually, I thought I'd go through some of Jack's stuff,' she said.

'Would you like some company?'

'No. No, thanks.'

She had listened to the talk of what a great man Jack had been as she circulated plates of sandwiches and sausage rolls amongst his drinking pals at the wake. 'We'll miss him down the White Horse,' from Charlie, the landlord. It was men like Jack who paid for his villa in Spain. And Terry Connolly from the Tara Club, 'He liked a flutter on the gee-gees, but don't we all?' A flutter was something that barely registered, like the flap of a butterfly's wings. It was more than a flutter the time two weeks' rent money galloped away on the back of a horse, and she and the children had to hide under the table when the rent man came, so he couldn't see them when he peered through the window. A flutter, was it? More like trying to hold your ground in the slipstream of a jumbo jet. She had to get a cleaning job at Long Grove to make up for that one: the hospital where she'd been training to be a nurse before she fell for Kieran.

'Jack was a man who enjoyed a drink,' even Father Westland mentioned it during the sermon at the funeral service. Jack enjoyed a drink while she enjoyed feeding five children and getting them off to bed; while she enjoyed keeping his dinner plate hot, on top of a saucepan of boiling water, until the water boiled dry. Sometimes he ate it when he came in, swaying at the kitchen counter. Other times it was still there in the morning, untouched, and she would scrape it into the dustbin.

She'd seen a film, *Spring and Port Wine,* where James

Mason made his wife serve up the same meal to their daughter for days. How she would have loved to do that, serve him the same meal every night of a weeklong drinking binge: cold pork chops, wizened peas and congealed gravy.

At the end of a binge, he would attempt to make amends – a box of Black Magic chocolates, a bunch of daffs or, the most romantic of all, an offering from the meat raffle at the White Horse. When the horses ran in the right direction, there would be money to treat herself and the kids, for a shopping trip to Kingston. They'd go to C&A and Chelsea Girl, and have lunch in Littlewoods café where there were photos on the wall of the meals you could choose, like the posters outside the pictures, stills from the main attraction, and you could pick them ready-plated from beneath hot lamps: fish, chips and peas; shepherd's pie and cabbage; lemon meringue pie with a fluted scoop of cream; apple tart and custard. No cooking, no washing up, and home on the 406 bus, laden with clothes and shoes and hats.

It was the children that kept her going throughout those years. She loved to watch them from the doorstep as they left for school or church, white socks for the girls, grey for the boys, hair washed and brushed, clothes ironed. And the school plays, the concerts, seeing them married, young Janice graduating from university.

Jack looked down at her, ageing from left to right, silver-framed on the mantelpiece: their wedding in black and white, the children's weddings in colour, and the last photo of him, taken at the Derby, his final win. A few more wrinkles to the right of the mantelpiece, but his eyes and his smile were the same.

It was his eyes and smile that made her fall for him the first time she met him at a dance above the Gas Showrooms in Epsom. She was slim then, before the children, red hair pinned up on the wards, but allowed to fall about her shoulders at the dances. She loved the dances, with the other Irish girls from the nurses' home, felt alive after the drudgery of the week. High heels and stockings, a good dress or a faithful skirt made to look new, with different blouses and scarves. She was wearing a new dress, powder blue, the night she met Jack. He was with a crowd she knew, but he was a fresh face, just arrived from Mitchelstown, County Cork. She'd never been beyond County Clare until she travelled to Dublin to catch the boat to Holyhead, but she'd seen the name on half-pounds of butter from the Mitchelstown Creamery – a smiling girl on the wrapper, mountains in the background – and Jack had a smile that would melt butter straight from the fridge.

So he walked her back to the nurses' home after the dance, and they started pairing off, his crowd and hers, going out all together or just the two of them. Summertime, it was, so her arms were bare for him to stroke as they kissed and cuddled, sometimes bare shoulders, and it was warm into September, so they took to walking on the common, picking blackberries, wandering into the woods as dusk fell.

She knew what was what, although she had never been told a thing by her mother; knew to keep private those parts of her that were private, but those eyes, that smile, the soft dusk of early autumn and the feel of his hands on her bare arms as they kissed, that's what did for her. Three months gone when they married, though you couldn't see from the photo, her bouquet held low, and she didn't show till late in her slimmer days.

Two became three, became four, became five, became six, until there were seven at the dinner table each evening. Then she fell for the last time. *Falling for a baby* made it sound like an accident: a gentle scrape of the knees. The sixth time it happened was more like hurtling from the skies without a parachute. Jack had the usual response to her pregnancy announcements: 'Not again.' She had given up hope of a scene like in the films, where the woman says, *Darling, I have something to tell you,* and the man says, *Oh Darling, are you?* Then the woman nods and smiles, and the man makes her sit down, put her feet up. None of them – Ronald Colman, Cary Grant, Jimmy Stewart – would have said, 'Not again.'

She was worn out, Doctor Stone said, couldn't cope with a sixth child; it would be for the best. 'And while we're at it, we'll get you sterilised.' Like a baby's bottle and teats floating in a tank of Milton's fluid.

There was no-one she could tell, no-one to confess to. Jack was shame-faced, tried to comfort her in the only way he knew, but that was what had got her into that state. Then he gave her money to get a nightie and a dressing gown for her stay in the District Hospital, and she went through the practicalities of buying them, packing her bag, and arranging for Joan to take charge of the children, only saying it was a gynae problem, and she'd be home in a week.

She allowed herself a few tears the night before the operation, as she lay without sleep, wondering should she slip from the bed, beyond the nurses' station and home; carry the sixth child to term. And she sat with a nurse, with a cup of tea, in the twilight of the day room with the light shining from the corridor. She was going to tell it all to the nurse, confess it to someone, but she accepted a sleeping pill instead.

Father Westland visited her on the ward, as she lay groggy and sore. 'I'll pray for you,' he said. 'See you at Mass when you're up and about.' But she was finished with that business and finished with the other business too. She would remain sterile, untouched. After the priest had gone, the words of the Agnus Dei ran through her head: *Agnus Dei, qui tollis peccata mundi, miserere nobis –*

Lamb of God, who takes away the sins of the world, have mercy on us.

She didn't know if Jack went elsewhere for it. She didn't want to know. At first she said she was recovering from the op. Then she made herself stay up late, so as not to go to bed at the same time as him. If she started to nod off, she'd step out the back door to wake up in the night air, and return to the late night telly until the national anthem played. She told Jack that she stayed up to see all the children in safely; Kieran and Maggie were teenagers by then. He tried, in his way, to put his arm about her, to kiss her, but he was met with a shoulder as stiff as a leg of lamb from the freezer, a cheek as receptive as Ted Heath was to the unions. After a while, he didn't trouble her anymore.

It was hard when each of the children left, when seven became six and so on. She would lay a place at the table, put a meal out for the missing child, and the laughter would start from the ones that were left: *Mum's done it again.* She would laugh along with them before retreating to the kitchen to wipe her eyes on a tea towel. Seven to six, to five, and then down to one. Some women expected their dead husbands to walk in at any time, but she knew that Jack was gone; no confusion that he might walk up the garden path at any time, fresh from the bookies or the White Horse.

She pulled back the curtain. The rain was clearing and the clouds shifted over to show the blue beneath. If only she lived near her children, then she could wander over for a cup of tea at this time of day. Or her grandchildren would sit being taught how to knit and sew, as she did with her own grandmother. Would they be interested, with their computers and video games? She picked up the phone and dialled Janice's number. It rang seven times then that voicemail contraption. Janice should be in; she had a workman coming round to fix the boiler. She switched off the talk button without leaving a message.

Janice was probably busy not being bored. Fancy declaring your marriage over due to boredom! No violence or mental cruelty, no drink or drugs or other women, no keeping her short of money: she was just bored with Phil. Maura would have relished boredom at her age, into her sixteenth year of motherhood with another dozen to go. Boredom would have been welcome.

She picked up the postcard from Jim-the-Milkman. She had looked forward to the clinking of the glass bottles on the milk float that announced his arrival every morning, all those years that Jack was out from first light to last orders, working on building sites around the country, or trailing round for work. No Job Centre or sending off CVs, just driving round with the others in the van, looking for sites, with the ever-hopeful greeting, 'Any chance of a start?' It was like being a widow with her husband still alive.

She and Jim-the-Milkman used to have coffee on the doorstep every morning when the weather was good. It wasn't the done thing to have him in the house; the neighbours would have talked. It wasn't what decent women did. But wouldn't it have been great to be Mrs Jim-the-Milkman, to have a husband home by lunchtime and an endless supply of dairy products? But you took what you were given in those days. No divorce, no get-out clause, no asking him to leave just because you were bored.

She'd never been to Tralee, though it wasn't that far from Clare, a jaunt across the Shannon. She hadn't been far at all as a young girl. As far as Lisdoonvarna to see her grandfather dying in the Stella Maris nursing home; as far as Doolin to catch the craic at a music session in the pubs; as far as Lahinch to get work in the hotels; as far as Dun Laoghaire with her suitcase containing two of everything to start a new life as a nurse in England. Tralee – all she knew of it was the song 'The Rose of Tralee'.

Tralee – it tripped off the tongue like a song: Tra-la-la, Tra-la-lee. The kind of place you could skip down the road singing and no-one would care. She turned over the card: *Waiting for your visit – come and have a coffee on my doorstep, Jim.* She picked up the Yellow Pages and turned to the Travel Agents section. 'What would I do with you, Lester Piggott, if I went swanning off to Tralee?' The dog raised his head and settled again, stretched across the back of the armchair. 'Maybe Joan would have you. Would you like that, Lester?' She settled into the chair, leaning so her head was cushioned by the dog's back. She flicked onto the opening credits of a Humphrey Bogart film on TCM, *To Have and Have Not.* The Yellow Pages remained open on the nest of tables, next to her coffee and cigarettes.

The Done Thing

Jan had been awake since five, humming Abba songs to block out the noises from Angie's bedroom in the house next door. As the grunts grew louder, Jan tried to focus on the blue plastic carriers that Angie would pass over the garden fence later on. Angie was dating Jerry Dallas – JR they called him. He had a stall on the market. Her fruit bowl was overflowing, more than she could handle, she said. Last weekend Angie had shared oranges and bananas along with a report on her progress with JR: *I don't want him living with me, but he's a good fuck.*

Angie had picked up JR in the Three Fishes. She never bought a drink for herself: she waited for one of the men to buy for her. Jan's mother said that women in pubs on their own were only after one thing. Jan drank alone, at home: white wine, maybe vodka. Vodka worked faster. Once in a while, when Phil had the girls and the house didn't answer back when she shouted, Jan went down the pub with Angie.

Jan was waiting for Kevin. She scanned the street for his Renault van through the rain-battered windowpanes she had cleaned the day before, and rubbed at a smear with her sleeve. She switched on the radio to clear her head of the stuttering lyrics of 'Take A Chance On Me'. It was tuned in to Capital Gold, seventies soul. She stripped the bed, shimmying to 'Let's Stay Together'. The back of her neck tingled with the memory of a hundred slow dances at Tiffany's nightclub, her arms draped around a boy's neck, his hands resting on her hips.

The tops that Angie had talked her into buying spilled out of the Primark bag on the floor. *I've told you, Jan, if you want to get a man you've got to start showing some tit.* She pulled off her sweatshirt and slipped on a pink, low-cut T-shirt with a ribbon of nylon lace around the neckline. She stood in front of the bedroom mirror, leaning forward. No-one about, time to kill, she drew the bedroom curtains, unzipped her jeans and pushed her fingers inside, kneading one of her breasts with the other hand. It never took long, always disappointed. She walked to the bathroom and scrubbed her crotch with a soapy flannel, which she added to the pile of sheets. She looked at herself once more, and buttoned a cardigan over her cleavage.

There weren't many men who towered over her, but Kevin was one of them. Six foot three, she'd say, lean. He reached to the top of the boiler casing like a dancer stretching. He lifted the panel, stripped it, in two smooth moves. He worked quietly, just the hiss of a transistor radio from the kitchen windowsill.

The kitchen floor was covered in tarpaulin. It looked like a picnic was about to be laid out. At one edge, an off-white canvas bag spilled tools over the tiles that she had swept and mopped after Phil had picked up the girls that morning. Kevin rejected and selected a succession of spanners, and lifted himself onto the worktop.

Jan unloaded the tumble drier, sorting knickers ranging from age ten to size fourteen. She rolled socks into pairs, each with a stitch of red or blue cotton on the inside for ease of matching. 'How long do you think it's going to take?' she asked. He shrugged. Kevin didn't give estimates of time, money, anything.

'Don't worry,' he said, his back turned. 'You worry too much. And you're always in a hurry. You know what I say? Don't dash.' He flashed a smile over his shoulder and lowered himself from the worktop onto the floor. He filled the kettle and picked two mugs from the cupboard. His fingers were long and slim; more suited to playing the piano than mending a boiler. 'Take this morning. It was raining, so I stayed indoors. When it rains, I don't work.'

She wanted to say that he wouldn't have got wet in her kitchen, mending the boiler, and that he hadn't phoned to say he'd be late. Instead, she took down the tin of Family Circle and laid some biscuits on a plate, two plain, two fancy. Jan thought of her mother; how she kept workmen sweet by giving them tea and coffee, but not until the job was well underway. It was part of her mother's rules, what was 'done' and what was 'not the done thing', like the way she used to make coffee for her friend, Jim-the-Milkman, when Jan was little; but he was never invited into the house.

Kevin turned the key in the back door and stepped out into the yard. He pulled the top of his overalls down so they hung from his waist as though another man was strapped to his back, arms dangling. He drew a cigarette from the pack of Benson and Hedges in his breast pocket, and placed it between his lips. She stopped herself from looking at the curve of his neck where it met his T-shirt. It reminded her of trying to look at Jim-the-Milkman without anyone noticing.

It was hard to look at Jim-the-Milkman without looking, but some people joked that Jan must be the milkman's daughter, and she wanted to know if it was true. Her brothers and sisters were blond or ginger, but Jan was dark, like Jim. He stopped every morning for a cup of Maxwell House, milk, three sugars. He sat on the left of the front doorsteps, on the red brick wall, and her mum sat on the wall on the other side of the door, with Jan close beside her.

It was rude to stare; Jan knew that, just like it was rude to write letters in red pen. It was one of those things that was not-the-done-thing. Asking her mum why it was not-the-done-thing was useless – either ignored or told, 'It just isn't,' with her back turned, peeling potatoes or dusting the china animals on the sideboard. One of those things that was half-explained, like why Jan shouldn't let the man from the Pru kiss her on the cheek when he came to collect the money on a Friday. She liked the man from the Pru; he spoke French to her. She was learning it at school – *Je m'appelle Jeanne* – Mrs Heath gave them all a French name. She mustn't be too nice to the man from the Pru, but she had to be nice to her dad's friend, Chozzy, even though he scared her. His real name was Charles Osbourne. When they went to the Irish Association dances he leaned over her with his whiskey-breath. It made sick come into her mouth, but she had to be nice to him. It was rude not to.

Some people didn't care about the done thing. They paid in kind, like that Mrs Oliver. She heard about them when Aunty Pam from across the road came in. Aunty Pam was not a real aunty, but a friend-of-the-family. She was allowed in the kitchen. That was the done thing, but not Jim-the-Milkman. If Jim-the-Milkman came in then her mum would be like that Mrs Oliver. It would be like letting the man from the Pru kiss her on the cheek: not-the-done-thing.

Her mum drank Maxwell House too – half milk, half water – and she and Jim-the-Milkman had a cigarette. Not fags, fags were common, like having a milk bottle on the table instead of a jug. Mum had Embassy cigarettes and Jim-the-Milkman smoked roll-ups. Jan watched his fingers pull tiny strands from the tin of Old Holborn and make feathery sausages. His fingers were orange.

Aunty Pam came over sometimes when Jim-the-Milkman was there. She had a big bosom. She held Jan close the day the dog died. Her bosom was springy when she pulled Jan's head into it. It smelt of an Avon talcum powder called *Occur!* Jan had tried out the talcum powder once, when she went to the loo at Aunty Pam's. Her mum had got cross, 'cause she'd made a mess with the powder puff, but Aunty Pam just laughed. She had seen Aunty Pam's bosom, all of it, at one of the Irish dances. It bounced out of her halter-neck dress during a dance called the 'Siege of Ennis'. Her mum said it was typical. Her mum told Aunty Joan that Aunty Pam and Uncle Dave were at it in the afternoons. Aunty Pam had answered the door with a red face, and Uncle Dave was on the stairs behind her, out of breath. Aunty Joan said there was nothing wrong with it. She and Uncle Bill went to bed on a Sunday afternoon, to catch up. Jan's mum said they were finished with all that business. Her dad went to bed by himself on a Sunday afternoon. Her mum fell asleep in front of the telly.

Kevin stubbed out his cigarette on the concrete of the back yard. 'We need some materials. You got some cash?'

'I'll come with you. I haven't been out all day.' She could pay by Visa, stretch her cash and, besides, she never saw the receipts when Kevin went alone.

She struggled with the door catch of the van when they reached All Bits plumbing supplies. 'Here, it's a bit dodgy,' he said. He reached across her, the outside of his

arm skimming her breast, took his time, his face close to
hers as he drew back to the driver's side. He set her ear-
ring dangling with the tip of his finger. 'They suit you,
your colour.'

The sweat on the back of Kevin's neck made his skin shine.
His hair was close-cropped, easy to manage, he said, when
he was doing dirty work. She wanted to touch it, to feel
the resistance of the tight curls springing against her hand.
His tongue pushed out from the corner of his mouth as he
worked.

'Coffee?'

His shoulders dropped, 'Oh, great.'

She used the good ground coffee that she kept in the
fridge, and laid the tray with a cafetière and a jug of milk.

'Mmm, real coffee.' His nostrils widened as she poured
the boiling water over the coffee grounds.

'You got much work on?'

'Oh, this and that.'

Handyman was a back-up; he had told her that the last
time he came. He had lots of back-ups, so he'd always
be in work, something his dad had taught him. He had
women back-ups too. His girlfriend knew. Men needed
back-ups, he'd said.

Kevin crossed the kitchen and pushed the plunger into
the coffee, his hands inches from hers. It was one year and
five days since Jan had touched a man, and she had only
ever touched four men: one at a time, no back-ups.

The DJ was playing 'My First, My Last, My Everything'
when Pete led her away from the flashing lights into the
woods behind St Joseph's Youth Club. He stuck his tongue
between her teeth when they kissed. It made her giggle.
Boys didn't like you laughing at them when they kissed
you. One hand down her knickers, he guided one of hers

beneath the soft snap of the elastic of his orange nylon underpants, her hand in his, up and down, up and down. She wiped her fingers with tissues from a pack of Handy Andies, and buried them beneath some leaves. It went on for months, on the common, in the park after the gates were shut. Going further, him promising he'd pull out in time, her counting the days between her periods. Vatican roulette: she was lucky she hadn't got caught. She wondered if her mum knew what she'd been up to when she went home, if she could tell by looking at her.

None of that worry once she married Phil; it was all right once you were married.

When there was cricket on the television, Phil slumped in front of it in the pose of a bored teenager. He never moved when the cricket was on, apart from the chewing of his bottom lip – to the left, then to the right. Year after year was the same, only the shape of his glasses changed – round then oblong with different prescriptions – but still the same position in front of the cricket, his pointed elbows angled either side of the armchair.

Sex was a once a fortnight, after *Match of the Day* in the football season, and whatever was on in its place in the cricket season. It was all you could expect, what married life was about. House, kids, car, holiday once a year, and sex once a fortnight.

Cliff came along soon after the break-up. He was a teacher at the girls' school; she'd chatted him up during a parents' evening. Months of creeping about, waiting until after the girls had gone to sleep. It couldn't go on, he said, the Head wouldn't like it: not the done thing.

Her last was a twenty-seven-year-old she'd met in the Three Fishes with Angie. He and his mate fancied her and her mate. That's how it was. Not much different from the discos at St Joseph's. They were working on the Channel Tunnel rail link, staying in a B&B, two lads away from home. He was good looking, nice eyes, a bit on the plump side, lived with his mum. He told her she was beautiful and kissed her neck. He made noises like an animal, howled. She came five times, a first – her first, her last. She binned the sheets afterwards, bought new ones at Matalan.

Kevin had finished the boiler and was cleaning the gutters. Rain had been pouring down the outside wall and seeping through the back door. There was always something. She could see his buttocks outlined in his overalls as she footed the ladder. She didn't let go when he came down the last few rungs, undid her buttons: one, two, three.

'I won't charge you for this; it's only taken ten minutes,' he said, detaching the upper rungs of the ladder, reducing it to half its length. He touched her arm. She took his hand and moved it to her breast. The phone was ringing inside the house. She counted: four, five, six. The voicemail would kick in after seven rings. She tilted her face towards his, towards the smell and the taste of coffee and smoke.

Self Help

Maggie had banished bleach from the house. She didn't share this with her mother who was searching for products to blitz Maggie's kitchen. She could see how the phrase 'keeping mum' had come about. She'd stopped telling her mother anything important as a teenager, and in the twenty-seven years since she'd left home, had learned to stick to safe subjects during her mother's visits. Her mother would, as she always did, fill the kitchen cupboard with toxic cleaning materials that Maggie would dump after she'd left. But the other thing, that something that Maggie needed to tell her, that wouldn't be resolved so easily.

Maggie practised the words she needed to say in her head as her mother balanced on a stool, a bucket of soapy water with a dash of vinegar in it on the ground. On the kitchen worktop was the slip of paper that the window cleaner had pushed through the letterbox the day before, to say that he had cleaned the very windows that she was polishing with balls of scrunched-up newspaper.

'You don't have to do this, Mum. You're on holiday,' Maggie said.

'Ah, it's no trouble at all. And you so busy with the job, and with Sarah still at home. I suppose you don't get the time to do it properly.' She climbed down from the stool, tipped the dirty water into the drain, then carried the bucket to the bathroom. 'Though it wouldn't hurt Sarah to do her bit; you had your chores when you were her age.'

'Her schoolwork is enough. Her GCSEs are coming up next year.'

'Qualifications are all well and good, but if she doesn't know how to run a house, she'll have trouble finding a husband.' She squirted Ecover spray on the tiles above the sink, and wrinkled her nose as it dribbled down. 'This is no good; you need something with bleach in it.'

'It's better for the environment, Mum.'

'That it might be, but it's no good for cleaning. Sarah!' she shouted into the hallway, 'I need you to go to the shops.' Maggie followed as her mother pushed into Sarah's bedroom, and flung the curtains open. 'What do you think you're doing, sitting indoors staring at that contraption, when it's a lovely day outside?'

Sarah stared at the screen of her laptop, fingers tapping at the keyboard. 'I'm talking to my friends on Messenger, Nan.'

'Well, I've a message for you. Here's what I need, and you can bring back cake and ice-cream.'

Sarah's complaints were to no avail as her Nan dictated the weird kind of list that Maggie herself had taken to Dolly's corner shop as a child – Flash with Bleach, J cloths, Jaffa Cakes – plus whatever cake and ice-cream she fancied.

The two women sorted through the cupboard under

the kitchen sink while Sarah was gone, discarding spray dispensers with fractions of inches of liquid in the bottom, throwing away tea towels that had seen better days, wiping the shelves of sticky circles and ovals where bottles had stood. Maggie waited for a chance to make eye contact. The self-help book that she was reading, *The Woman You Are*, said eye contact was the key to communication. The author had obviously never encountered Maggie's mother, who tended to talk with her back turned, head bowed, busy with some task or other. Just as there was a pause in activity, a gap in the constant chatter, Sarah came back with the shopping, and the cleaning of the bathroom began.

'These tiles will come up lovely now. You've got to have the proper tools for the job, Maggie.' Her right hand circled the wall, a cloth grasped in it; a one-woman cleaning windmill, armed with products guaranteed to kill 99% of all known germs and a range of wildlife to boot once it entered the water system. She was standing in the bath, barefoot in bra and slip, discarding clothes as she grew hotter, reaching higher, disturbing the cobwebs in the corner as she worked. *Replace the impulse with something else, some other words or action,* the self-help book said. 'Coffee?' Maggie said, to stop the scream in her head escaping.

'In a minute, when I've done these taps.'

Maggie kept a jar of Mellow Birds for when her mother visited: coffee for people who didn't like coffee. She'd be better off with something herbal – a camomile infusion – but when Maggie had made one on her last visit, her mother had declared it to be 'muck'.

She stepped out of the bath, hair wild, face flushed, and sipped at her coffee. She grimaced. 'Too strong, Maggie. A dash more milk.' She held the cup out to her daughter.

'Do you want to put your blouse and skirt back on, Mum?'

'Ah, it's only us. All girls together.'

Maggie had always found her mother's habit of semi-nudity in the house difficult to understand: so prudish when referring to 'private parts' or 'the monthly visitor', yet happy to walk round the house in bra and slip when there were no men around. Maggie lifted her mother's blouse off the hook on the back of the bathroom door, and handed it to her.

'All right, but only because I need to go out for some Domestos for the toilet. That thin stuff you use is no good.'

Replace the impulse with something else, some other words or action. 'I thought we'd go to Bluewater tomorrow, make a day of it.'

'That new shopping centre? Oh, I've heard it's great!' A smile at last. 'What shall I wear?' She headed for the spare room to hunt through her suitcase, the Domestos now forgotten.

Maggie used to argue about the cleaning, the fault-finding, before she read *The Woman You Are*. The book had a mirrored cover, which you could look at to give yourself some *positive self-talk*. Before her mother's visit, she'd talked herself into looking on the bright side: it was like having a team of professional cleaners in for free, and it made her mother feel useful. And if there were subjects that needed broaching, as there were now, the best time to talk was not when Maggie was annoyed and her mother in the throes of a cleaning frenzy. *Choose a quiet time and make eye contact,* the book said. She just wished that her mother would stay still and stop talking for long enough.

The cup of Mellow Birds stood by the bathroom sink with less than half an inch drunk from it. It was tepid. Maggie steadied herself, a hand on the sink, then locked the bathroom door. She stared into the mirror on the medicine cabinet, and mouthed the words at her reflection. She hadn't said them out loud yet, and they stuck below her throat as though the hole that would let them through had been stitched shut. She splashed her face with cold water, unlocked the door, and took the cup to the kitchen. She made a fresh coffee for her mother, less strong and with more milk. 'Courage,' she said out loud: one of the affirmations that the book suggested. She climbed the stairs to the spare room, which her mother made her own during her visits.

Home and Away was blaring from the small television set perched on the chest of drawers. It was usually kept in the kitchen, but moving it upstairs stopped Maggie from being subjected to a continuous diet of soaps, and Sarah could watch *Hollyoaks* in the living room, without her grandmother commenting on the scanty clothes the girls wore. Maggie's mother was stretched out on the bed, propped up on pillows. She barely turned her head as Maggie placed her coffee on the bedside table, then perched on the edge of the bed. 'I can't see, Maggie.'

Maggie shifted. 'I thought we could have a chat.'

'Not while my programmes are on.'

Maggie thought of turning off the television, of forcing the conversation, but her courage disappeared below the stitched-up hole where the words were hiding. It was a relief, in a way, to keep mum a little longer. They'd talk after their shopping trip. Why spoil the day for everyone? And perhaps things wouldn't turn out so badly; maybe there would be no need to tell her at all. 'Okay,' she said, 'I'll leave you to it, and make a start on the dinner.'

Maggie could hear the television from the room above the kitchen as she chopped onions for the casserole. She wondered if her mother was going deaf. Her father was the one for turning up the telly and the radio. He'd have the wireless, as he called it, at full volume when he got up at five for work when she was small. She'd got used to it, to waking with a start to a booming BBC voice, then dozing through it, woken again when he switched off the radio and left the house. The silence was hard to sleep through after he'd gone, the lull before the rest of the house rose, and she'd lay on one side, legs drawn up to her chest, making up poems in her head. But he had genuine deafness to contend with, from years of noise on building sites in the days when no-one wore ear defenders. Maybe her mother had the telly loud in memory of him; like when Maggie stayed with her Nan after her Grandad had died, and they watched the wrestling on *World of Sport;* not because her Nan liked it, but that was what they watched on a Saturday afternoon, when her Grandad was alive.

There was a gap between *Neighbours* and *Coronation Street* when Maggie could have had that chat with her mother, but then John came home from work, and with all four of them at the table, there was no chance to talk to her mother alone.

'That mattress is lumpy,' Maggie's mother said. 'And the pillows are as flat... I've a terrible ache in my neck.' Maggie placed a glass of water and a pack of Nurofen next to her mother's breakfast bowl. For most of her life she'd *got on with things,* a quiet martyr whose frowns, and what Maggie and her sisters called *bad moods,* were the only clues to illness or unhappiness. Then came *the change,* and the change was that a woman who had cooked Christmas dinner suffering with the flu one year, holding onto a kitchen worktop with one hand as she stirred the gravy with the other, now clung onto aches and pains like she'd tried to hang on to each of her children as they left home.

'My arthritis is playing up. Would you open the packet for me, Maggie?'

Maggie had read that arthritis was the body holding onto distress from the past, that a good counsellor would get rid of it. She had tried telling her mother once. 'Counselling, is it? I raised the five of you without a counsellor, and with your father the way he was.' So she had learned to keep quiet, and keep a good supply of painkillers next to the jar of Mellow Birds.

'Are you sure you're up to going to Bluewater? It's a lot of walking.'

'Ah, I'll be fine.' She took a plastic box from her handbag. It was divided into a grid of squares with columns marked with the days of the week and rows of *Morning, Lunchtime* and *Evening.* She tipped the pills from one of the squares into her hand and swallowed each of them, then two Nurofen. 'I could buy you some new pillows while we're there; my treat.'

Sarah did not wish to be roused from her half-term bed. In term-time, Maggie could get her up and dressed, get a load of washing done, then drop her at school before going on to work; it was impossible to leave the house before eleven in the holidays. When Sarah did get up, she sat on the sofa in her pyjamas, eating toast, watching an episode of *Friends* on Channel 4. Meanwhile, Maggie's mother scoured all the cups in the kitchen with Vim. 'That dishwasher doesn't really get them clean.' She then put all the kitchen cloths into a bucket of neat bleach, having remembered the need for Domestos late the evening before, sending John out to buy some. 'Oh, my back is in a terrible state from that bed,' she said as she emptied a load of washing from the machine and hauled the plastic basket out to the garden. She had rinsed her tights and knickers from the previous day by hand after breakfast, and they were already dripping on the rotary clothes line.

'Come on, that's enough telly for this morning,' Maggie said as one episode of *Friends* ended, with another promised after the break.

'I know how to get her moving.' Maggie's mother opened her purse.

'Mum, please.'

'If your grandmother can't treat you, then who can?' She walked into the living room, a twenty pound note in her hand. 'Come on now, time to get ready, and this is for you to buy whatever you want.' Sarah reached up and took the money.

'What do you say, Sarah?' Maggie said.

'Thanks, Nan.' She rose and gave her grandmother a hug, before sinking back down on the sofa, curling her legs beneath her.

'None of that, young lady; upstairs with you and get dressed.' The older woman hauled her granddaughter up by the arm and guided her to the stairs.

'You have to be firm, Maggie. I know your youngest will always be your baby. I know what it's like when your children leave, and you want to hold on to the last one to go, but you're spoiling her, letting her spend half the day in her pyjamas.'

'At least I don't try to buy her affection.'

'I usually treat her when I come to stay.'

'But you could have bought her something when we were out, rather than bribing her to get ready.'

'Bribing is it? So I'm not allowed to give her anything without your permission?' She looked wounded.

Maggie wanted to stamp her feet, the logic of her argument lost as the courage she'd been summoning all night and all morning shifted to rage within seconds. She took a deep breath. 'Sorry, Mum. Let's not start the day on the wrong foot.'

'I should think you are sorry. I come all this way to visit, and you speak to me like this.' She rummaged for a tissue in her handbag.

You can't change other people; you can only change yourself. 'Look, I'm sorry I upset you. We'll have a lovely day – you, me and Sarah. All girls together, eh?' She squeezed her mother's arm.

'If we can ever get that girl out of the door.'

'Heads and shoulders, knees and toes', the song went through Maggie's head as she heard her mother's catalogue of headache, sore shoulder and twinges in the knee from the passenger seat of the car, then Sarah asking if she could have some Vans when they got to Bluewater.

'What would you be doing with a van, Sarah. You're not old enough to drive.'

'Vans are trainers, Nan.' There was a giggle from the back seat. 'I could do with some new bras, too, Mum.'

'It's eggcups you'll be wanting,' her grandmother said.

Maggie remembered the mortification of being the last girl in her class to get a bra, whilst Debbie Dolan paraded round the changing rooms after swimming, chest thrust out in a Teenform training bra. Her mother liked to boast about her own 'bosoms', that they stayed firm into middle age by wearing bras night and day. Maggie remembered the roll-ons, rubber panties that her mother wriggled into by day, and a full set of underwear worn under her nightie. It was a miracle that she didn't have permanent thrush. And that her father got through all of that to give her five children. She wondered if her father had ever seen her mother naked, or if he just pulled aside a gusset. She stifled a giggle at the thought of her mother giving birth with her knickers still on.

'We'll go bra shopping another day, Sarah. Just the two of us.'

There was tutting over the price of the Vans and comments on everything Sarah tried on. Sarah took off by herself as soon as she got the clothes she wanted, promising to meet up later. 'Ah well, some time to ourselves,' Maggie's mother said, linking arms as they went into House of Fraser. Maybe this would be the time to talk, when they were in public, and there wouldn't be a scene. Or maybe there would be, and Maggie would have to deal with it.

Her aches and pains were forgotten, as Maggie's mother marvelled at the size of each of the stores in turn, and the range of pillows offered by John Lewis. She attacked shopping with the same gusto as she had the bathroom tiles, and went into ecstasy about the changing rooms in M&S: 'They make you feel like a film star.' Maggie followed in her wake, carrying bulging bags of pillows, taped together at the handles. She dropped them in a chair next to her mother in the Revive café, and left her there whilst she queued at the counter. She formed the words that she needed to say in her head as the queue inched forward, changed the order of them.

'Sarah should be here by now,' Maggie said. Their cups lay empty next to side plates with cake crumbs and crumpled paper serviettes. Her phone beeped a text from Sarah: *Mtg Holly and Nathan @ 2. Will get bus home l8r.* She read it to her mother.

'That's a shame. I suppose it's a bit boring for her, spending time with an old granny.'

Maggie wanted to tell her that if she hadn't given Sarah the twenty pound note, she'd have had her company a little longer. *Replace the impulse with something else, some other words or action.* 'Shall we have another coffee?' she said.

'This stuff gives me heartburn.'

'Try decaff.'

'De-what?'

'It's the caffeine that gives you heartburn, sends you racing, then drops you into a slump.'

'I'm fine with my Mellow Birds.'

They fell quiet. Maybe now was the time to tell her. It would be easier without Sarah there.

'Let me treat you to something, Mum.'

'Sure, what do I need at my age?'

'A new top, a handbag? How about that vase we saw in John Lewis?' She'd seen her mother hover by the vase, then pick it up and turn it, holding it up to the light.

'Ah, I'm not that keen on cut flowers, Maggie.'

Maggie remembered the disdainful looks at the bunches of daffs and tulips on Mothers' Day. Her mother preferred pot plants, rose bushes for the garden that you could buy from Woolworth's with the roots wrapped in plastic. There was something about cut flowers that made her sad. She couldn't enjoy them in their best bloom, accept that they were a thing of beauty for a few short days. She wanted plants that she could work at, growing, feeding, weeding, pruning. A garden wasn't to be sat in and enjoyed. Work was her pleasure; working till she dropped.

'How's the garden, Mum?'

'I'm not able to do what I used to, with the arthritis.'

'Would Brendan help?' Her brother lived closest, had been the closest.

'He's not interested in gardening.' She shifted in her seat, reached into her bag, pulled out and unwrapped a Rennie.

'He'd help if you asked, him and Ian.'

'His friend? Why would he want to help?'

'His boyfriend, Ian's his boyfriend.'

'Hush!' She blushed, looked around, and hunched her shoulders over her empty coffee cup. 'Go and get another coffee, Maggie.' She pushed a five pound note across the table.

'I thought you didn't like the coffee.' Her mother zipped her purse and focused deep into her handbag as she put it away.

Maggie weaved through the tables to join the queue. People engaged in conversation, slumped over their drinks with bags advertising various stores on the seats beside them; single people checking their phones or reading the triangular columns of cardboard with information about the Fairtrade products in this café; *Mind if I join you* signals, and open-palmed gesturing into seats; the strained conversations of strangers. She wanted to be one of them, with anyone but her mother.

A woman behind the hot drinks machine asked her what she'd like. Her mouth wouldn't open. She left her tray on the metal runners with the five pound note resting on it, and walked back to the table.

'Where's the coffee, Maggie?'

Maggie's legs wouldn't bend for her to sit down. Her mother looked up at her.

'Maggie, whatever's the matter? You're as white as a sheet.'

Maggie made eye contact with her mother. The hole in her throat opened up and the words came out: 'Mum, I've got cancer.'

Combing out the Tangles

They don't allow cut flowers and, in any case, I don't know why you'd want to be lying there watching them shrivel. There'd be no room for them on those tiny lockers, let alone the risk of whatever the reason is that they're banned. Three beds to a bay when there should only be two, cards stuck to the wall with Blu Tack. I couldn't pick out a card in the League of Friends shop, let alone think of what to write. So I brought the practical things – tissues, barley water, wet wipes for when she got hot. And the comb; I left her the comb.

Dickens Ward she was in, my Maggie, down in the bowels of the hospital. I shuddered when I stepped out of the lift, walked the corridor underground. It didn't do much for patient morale, nor that of the visitors. Yet I managed a smile as I saw her, and she gave one in return. I drew the curtain for a bit of privacy. The bay was so small that the shape of me bulged through the curtain.

They'd given her a shower that morning, and she was in the new jeans that John had brought in for her, as she'd gone down a few sizes. Her legs were lost in them, but still they wouldn't do up over her swollen belly. I could see the bones of her clavicle where the flesh had lost its plumpness, her throat sunken. She reminded me of one of those children in Biafra, back when she was at St Joseph's. She'd brought an envelope home – pennies for the black babies – went round collecting change from me and her father, from the neighbours, brought this bulging envelope back to school.

Her hair had been towel-dried and left any-old-how, so I said, 'Shall I brush your hair?' but I couldn't find her hairbrush in the locker. I'd a comb in my bag. It'd been there so long it was clogged with fluff and bits of tissue, but I picked it clean, washed it in the sink in the toilets, propped her up and started combing.

'That feels lovely,' she said as I combed first her fringe, then the one side of her hair. Her style had grown out. She kept it short, as a rule, and it was in need of a trim. I worked gently. She looked so fragile. Then there were knots and tangles at the back of her head. It was an effort for her to lean forward, to support her own weight. 'Give it a good old go, Mum,' she said, and I pulled a little harder, taking pressure from the roots, clipping my fingers like a clothes peg above where the comb was pulling.

'I hadn't the patience for this when you were little,' I said. I'd Kieran already when Maggie was born, Sharon followed soon after, then Brendan and Janice. 'It was a quick rub with the towel, and the comb dragged through where it would go.'

She chuckled. 'Your fingers felt like they'd go through my skull when you washed my hair.'

'Brisk and efficient, that's me.' I smiled.

'Never get a proper wash at the hairdresser's. Not

compared to you.'

'I know. They just won't dig their fingers in your scalp. Scared you'll prosecute them for assault.'

She leaned sideways and spat dark blood into one of the papier mâché bowls stacked on the bed table. Then she leaned back on the pillows and closed her eyes.

She had always been a big girl, tall like her father, big-breasted like me; now like parchment stretched over bones, and her bosoms shrivelled to nothing. I thought of holding her hand, but it wasn't something we did, so I laid a palm on her head as she slept as I used to when she was a baby. Her hair was brittle, like shredded wheat. It had been so full and hard to tame, a lion's mane, her crowning glory. Her mouth was agape as she slept, the slightest of breath coming from it. I wanted to lie down alongside her, feel her body against me as I had when I cradled her forty-odd years before, but the ward was too full of noise and people, beds being moved as patients came and went, and the sound of someone talking on the phone in the next bed, having a row with her boyfriend.

She didn't come to before the end of visiting time. I told a nurse I'd left her the comb, that I wasn't through tidying Maggie's hair, and asked could she do it. I doubt she'd the time for such niceties.

They moved her into a side room the day after. Unrestricted visiting, but I didn't go back. John said she kept sending him and the children to the canteen to bring her bits of food: jacket potatoes, jelly, cups of coffee, a packet of Quavers one time. She thought if she could eat a little then they'd start the treatment again. Not a bite stayed down. In the end, the Macmillan nurses came and spoke to her, so she could let go.

John called at seven this morning. She'd left us in the early hours, but he didn't want to wake me. Not that I'd slept a wink. I said I'd get on the phone to her sisters and brothers, but when it came to it, I couldn't say the words when I called Kieran, but he knew. He said he'd call the others, then he's coming over to drive me to Chatham.

I'll need an overnight bag. John will want me to stay to help with the arrangements. So much to do. It's the busy-ness that keeps you going, stops you thinking. I wonder did that nurse comb her hair after all. I wonder what they did with the comb.

Notes and Acknowledgements

These stories were five years in the making, starting with a pair of stories: early versions of 'The Done Thing' and 'A Coffee and a Smoke'. Thanks to Patricia Debney who read them and noticed that, more than anything, I needed to write more to discover where I had come from. Thanks to Susan Wicks for her criticism and encouragement during and beyond my time under her tutorship at the University of Kent. I must also thank Julia Bell and Martina Evans for an excellent tutored retreat with the Arvon Foundation in 2010, at a time when I was ready to give up on these stories. Thanks also to numerous writing friends for their support and constructive comments over the years, to my family in England and Ireland, and especially to my husband Bob.

I would like to acknowledge the assistance of bursaries from the Arvon Foundation and Swale Arts Forum during the writing of these stories, as well as a grant from Lawlor Foundation, which enabled me to study for a Certificate and later an MA in creative writing.

Amongst my reading, when writing these stories, were these books: *Across the Water, Irish Women's Lives In Britain*, M. Lennon, M. McAdam and J. O'Brien (Virago, 1988); *Goodbye to Catholic Ireland*, Mary Kenny (Templegate, 2000); and *Are you Somebody?* Nuala O'Faolain (Sceptre, 1997). Like many of the books I read, these were found in charity shops.

The idea for 'More Katharine than Audrey' came from 'Life Sentence', Angus Stickler's report for BBC Radio 4's *Today* programme, broadcast on 28 July 2008, on the women typhoid carriers locked up for many years in Long Grove mental hospital, Epsom, the town where I grew up.

'A Tea Party' was published on the website of *Tales of the Decongested* and read at their event at Foyles bookshop, London, in January 2008. It was also winner of the Save As Prose Awards, 2011, and published on the Save As Writers' website.

'Cold Salt Water' was winner of the Save As Prose Awards, 2009, and was published in *The Frogmore Papers*, Issue 75, Spring 2010 and in the anthology *Unexplored Territory*, edited by Maria C. McCarthy, Cultured Llama 2012.

'More Katharine than Audrey' and 'As Long as it Takes' were published on the website *Writers' Hub*, February 2011 and November 2011, respectively.

Cultured Llama Publishing

hungry for poetry
thirsty for fiction

Cultured Llama was born in a converted stable. This creature of humble birth drank greedily from the creative source of the poets, writers, artists and musicians that visited, and soon the llama fulfilled the destiny of its given name.

Cultured Llama is a publishing house, a multi-arts events promoter and a fundraiser for charity. It aspires to quality from the first creative thought through to the finished product.

www.culturedllama.co.uk

Also published by Cultured Llama

A Radiance
by Bethany W. Pope

Paperback; 70pp; 203x127mm;
978-0-9568921-3-3; June 2012
Cultured Llama

Family stories and extraordinary images glow throughout this compelling debut collection from an award-winning author, like the disc of uranium buried in her grandfather's backyard. *A Radiance* 'gives glimpses into a world both contemporary and deeply attuned to history – the embattled history of a family, but also of the American South where the author grew up.'

> 'A stunning debut collection ... these poems invite us to reinvent loss as a new kind of dwelling, where the infinitesimal becomes as luminous as ever.'
>
> Menna Elfyn

'*A Radiance* weaves the voices of four generations into a rich story of family betrayal and survival, shame and grace, the visceral and sublime. A sense of offbeat wonder at everyday miracles of survival and love both fires these poems and haunts them – in a good way.'

Tiffany S. Atkinson

'An exhilarating and exceptional new voice in poetry.'

Matthew Francis

Also published by Cultured Llama

strange fruits
by Maria C. McCarthy

Paperback; 72pp; 203x127mm;
978-0-9568921-0-2; July 2011
Cultured Llama (in association with
WordAid.org.uk)

Maria is a poet of remarkable skill, whose work offers surprising glimpses into our 21st-century lives – the 'strange fruits' of our civilisation or lack of it. Shot through with meditations on the past and her heritage as 'an Irish girl, an English woman', *strange fruits* includes poems reflecting on her urban life in a Medway town and as a rural resident in Swale.

Maria writes, and occasionally teaches creative writing, in a shed at the end of her garden.

All profits from the sale of *strange fruits* go to Macmillan Cancer Support, Registered Charity Number 261017.

'Maria McCarthy writes of the poetry process: "There is a quickening early in the day" ('Raising Poems'). A quickening is certainly apparent in these humane poems, which are both natural and skilful, and combine the earthiness and mysteriousness of life. I read *strange fruits* with pleasure, surprise and a sense of recognition.'

Moniza Alvi

Canterbury Tales on a Cockcrow Morning
by Maggie Harris

Paperback; 136pp; 203x127mm;
978-0-9568921-6-4; September 2012
Cultured Llama

Maggie Harris brings warmth and humour to her *Canterbury Tales on a Cockcrow Morning* and tops them with a twist of calypso.

Here are pilgrims old and new: Eliot living in 'This Mother Country' for half a century; Samantha learning that country life is not like in the magazines.

There are stories of regret, longing and wanting to belong; a sense of place and displacement resonates throughout.

> 'Finely tuned to dialogue and shifting registers of speech, Maggie Harris' fast-moving prose is as prismatic as the multi-layered world she evokes. Her Canterbury Tales, sharply observed, are rich with migrant collisions and collusions.'

John Agard

The Strangest Thankyou
by Richard Thomas

Paperback; 98pp; 203x127mm;
978-0-9568921-5-7; October 2012
Cultured Llama

Richard Thomas's debut poetry collection embraces the magical and the mundane, the exotic and the everyday, the surreal rooted in reality.

Grand poetic themes of love, death and great lives are cut with surprising twists and playful use of language, shape, form and imagery.

The poet seeks 'an array of wonder' in "Dig" and spreads his 'riches' throughout *The Strangest Thankyou.*

> 'He has long been one to watch, and with this strong, diverse collection Richard Thomas is now one to read. And re-read.'

Matt Harvey

Also published by Cultured Llama

Unauthorised Person
by Philip Kane

Paperback; 74pp; 203x127mm;
978-0-9568921-4-0; November 2012
Cultured Llama

Philip Kane describes *Unauthorised Person* as a 'concept album' of individual poems, sequences, and visuals, threaded together by the central motif of the River Medway.

This collection draws together poems written and images collected over 27 years, exploring the psychogeography of the people and urban landscapes of the Medway Towns, where 'chatham high street is paradise enough' ("johnnie writes a quatrain").

> 'This collection shows a poet whose work has grown in stature to become strong, honest and mature. Yet another voice has emerged from the Medway region that I'm sure will be heard beyond our borders. The pieces here vary in tone, often lyrical, sometimes prosaic but all show a deep rooted humanity and a political (with a small p) sensibility.'

Bill Lewis

Unexplored Territory
edited by Maria C. McCarthy

Paperback; 112pp; 203x127mm;
978-0-9568921-7-1; November 2012
Cultured Llama

Unexplored Territory is the first anthology from
Cultured Llama – poetry and fiction that take a
slantwise look at worlds, both real and imagined.

Contributors:

Jenny Cross	Philip Kane	Hilda Sheehan
Maggie Drury	Luigi Marchini	Fiona Sinclair
June English	Maria C. McCarthy	Jane Stemp
Maggie Harris	Rosemary McLeish	Richard Thomas
Mark Holihan	Gillian Moyes	Vicky Wilson
Sarah Jenkin	Bethany W. Pope	

'A dynamic range of new work by both established and
emerging writers, this anthology offers numerous delights.

The themes and preoccupations are wide-ranging. Rooted
in close observation, the poems and short fiction concern the
'unexplored territory' of person and place.

A must for anyone who likes good writing.'

Nancy Gaffield
author of *Tokaido Road*

The Night My Sister
Went to Hollywood
by Hilda Sheehan

Paperback; 82pp; 203x127mm;
978-0-9568921-8-8; March 2013
Cultured Llama

In *The Night My Sister Went To Hollywood* Hilda Sheehan offers poems on love, exhaustion, classic movies, supermarket shopping and seals in the bathtub. Her poems 'bristle with the stuff of life'. Her language is 'vigorous and seductively surreal'. 'What kind of a mother writes poems / anyway, and why?' she asks. A mother of five, Hilda Sheehan is that kind of mother. Read this debut poetry collection now: 'time is running out ... Asda will shut soon'.

I was constantly impressed by a sense of voice, and a wonderful voice, clear and absolutely achieved. Throughout ... domestic imagery makes of the kitchen and the household tasks a contemporary epic. The deceptively trivial detail of our daily lives works just as in Dickens, a great collector of trivia, and the pre-Raphaelites, revealing a powerful gift for metaphor. As Coleridge said, metaphor is an important gift of the true poet, and Hilda Sheehan has that gift in abundance.

William Bedford
author of *Collecting Bottle Tops: Selected Poetry 1960-2008*

It's one thing to have a vivid imagination. It's another to be adept at language. It's quite another to be gifted with the language to release and express that imagination. Hilda Sheehan has all three. She has the ability to see the pathos – as well as the joie de vivre – in the human comedy, and to convey it in a vigorous and sometimes seductively surreal language. We are enabled to see what we may not have been able or prepared to see, or even thought of seeing: this is what poetry is all about.

Robert Vas Dias
author of *Still-Life and Other Poems of Art and Artifice*

Notes from a Bright Field
by Rose Cook

Paperback; 104pp; 203x127mm;
978-0-9568921-9-5; July 2013
Cultured Llama

Rose Cook's *Notes From a Bright Field* is 'a single quiet
path, in and out', capturing the transitory beauties
of the everyday: a mother's ashes imagined as 'Lux flakes'; the 'fruit-
gummed glass' of a cathedral. Where the poems' themes are of nature,
loss and the spiritual, these are grounded in concrete imagery like 'the
clack-clack of the shell and the bones'.

In their transparency and deceptive simplicity Rose Cook's
poems reveal pure and hidden depths in nature, memory and
loss, celebrating and questioning the fragility of everyday inter-
actions. These are indeed poems for people 'who juggle [their]
lives', insisting in their gratitude that we 'be still sometimes'.
To read *Notes From a Bright Field* is to be renewed in body, mind
and spirit.

Anthony Wilson
author of *Riddance*

Rose Cook's poems are often poignant, reflecting the many vari-
ables of ordinary lives, but always with a lightness of touch, an
acceptance of what it is to be human. A collection fluid and sin-
cere, the poems are wide ranging, sometimes painterly, sometimes with a wonderful down-to-earth diction and a singular
inwardness that delights.

Denise McSheehy
author of *Salt*

Sounds of the Real World
by Gordon Meade

Paperback; 104pp; 203x127 mm;
978-0-9926485-0-3; August 2013
Cultured Llama

Sounds of the Real World is partly a bestiary, where man
and creature are 'separated by nothing but a pane of
glass'. The sea is 'a simmer in a pan' throughout, charting the poet's
move from his native Scotland to inner city London. Gordon Meade
is not just standing and staring at nature; these poems offer social
commentary as well as candid reflections on relationships, memory
and mortality.

> The vicissitudes of tide and weather, the creatures that are his
> motifs – from the slugs ground under his father's heel to the
> ghostly gorillas at Heidelberg Zoo – and the vagaries of his own
> heredity ... all are depicted with clarity and vitality, the familial
> poems instilling a sense of lurking unease.
>
> Stewart Conn
> author of *The Breakfast Room*

> You expect a new book of poems by Gordon Meade to be full
> of weather, birds, fish and animals (including humans). *Sounds
> of the Real World* doesn't disappoint. In his deceptively simply
> matter-of-fact, sharply observant way, Meade delineates our
> relationship with the natural world and with each other, adding
> a dollop of zen wisdom. And running through the book is
> Meade's passion, the sea, like life both 'wavering and constant'.
>
> Hamish Whyte
> author of *The Unswung Axe*

> To read Gordon Meade's poems is to feel you've met the man,
> walked and talked with him and shared his way of looking at the
> world with an acutely observant eye and a wry and imaginative
> mind. A poet who is a life companion.
>
> Diana Hendry
> author of *Late Love & Other Whodunnits*

Lightning Source UK Ltd.
Milton Keynes UK
UKOW03f1030290114

225467UK00002B/4/P